Laney looked long and hard at the lines on her father's face and frowned at the thinness of his gray hair.

Being a sheriff meant everything to him. Without the job, some essential part of him might die. He wasn't the type to sit home and watch ball games on TV. He had no hobbies, and his friendships grew out of work.

As her glance widened to include her brothers, she saw the open skepticism on their faces. They saw her as their little sister, softhearted and scatterbrained. Here was an opportunity to show how wrong they were.

Thomas cleared his throat, gently prodding her for an answer. Words either to accept or decline clogged her throat.

Beside her, Rock vibrated with excitement. Finally, unable to contain himself any longer, he shot to his feet, spilling iced tea from his raised glass.

"Of course she'll do it!" Rock cried. "A toast to the star of G. C.'s campaign!"

As everyone toasted Laney's success, Angel heaved a long-suffering sigh. Putting his head on his front paws, the little dog closed his eyes as if to say it was all too much for him.

KIM O'BRIEN grew up in Bronxville, New York, with her family and many pets—fish, cats, dogs, gerbils, guinea pigs, parakeets, and even a big thoroughbred horse named Pops. She worked for many years as a writer, editor, and speechwriter for IBM in New York. She holds a masters of fine arts in writing from Sarah Lawrence College in New York and is active in the Fellowship of The Woodlands church. She lives in The Woodlands, Texas, with her husband, two daughters, and, of course, pets.

The Pastor's Assignment

Kim O'Brien

Heartsong Presents

To Mike, Beth, and Maggie, who make my world a pretty great place to be, and to our heavenly Father, who makes all things possible.

A note from the Author:
I love to hear from my readers! You may correspond with me by writing:

Kim O'Brien
Author Relations
PO Box 719
Uhrichsville, OH 44683

ISBN 1-59310-522-3

THE PASTOR'S ASSIGNMENT

Our mission is to publish and distribute inspirational products offering exceptional value and biblical encouragement to the masses.

All scripture quotations are taken from the King James Version of the Bible.

All of the characters and events in this book are fictitious. Any resemblance to actual persons, living or dead, or to actual events is purely coincidental.

PRINTED IN THE U.S.A.

one

"You don't have to be perfect for God to love you perfectly." Pastor Bruce Burke raised his arms as if in confirmation from above. Hundreds of eyes followed his gaze to settle on the basketball scoreboard above his head. Although Good Faith Community was one of the largest churches in Destiny, Texas, it was also one without its own building. Sunday services were held in the gymnasium of the local high school.

"If you will take out the yellow insert in your bulletin," the pastor continued, "I'd like you to jot down your deepest regrets. We're going to ask God to take away our regrets."

Laney Varner reached inside the parrot-green straw bag at her feet. She smiled at Cinderella's likeness on the pen then clicked the spring and listened with astonishment as strains of "Someday My Prince Will Come" played softly but audibly in the silent gym.

Heads swiveled to see who was playing the music. Under the weight of their stares, Laney squirmed and wished her folding chair would swallow her. Pen in hand, she prayed the music would stop. Not only did it continue, but it also seemed to grow louder. She had to do something. With as much poise as she could muster, she sat on the pen.

She folded her hands in her lap and tried to pretend she

didn't hear the muted notes rising beneath her. Her seven-year-old niece must have slipped the pen inside her purse the last time she'd babysat her.

Next to her, Rock, her fiancé, solemnly handed her a pen and shook his head sadly. His nostrils flared, and his dark green eyes rolled as he let out a long-suffering sigh.

Blushing, Laney half-smiled in apology and concentrated fiercely on the pen in her hands. For a moment the sparkle of her diamond caught her eye. She frowned at it, never quite used to seeing it on her finger.

She recalled how, in the space between Rock's proposal and her sudden intake of breath, the ring had been planted firmly on her finger. If his proposal lacked sentimentality, Laney attributed it to Rock's job. As a district attorney, Rock was happier dealing with facts than feelings and more comfortable arguing for jail sentences than holy matrimony.

Laney's hair fell forward across her face, hiding the color she was sure must be blazing in her cheeks. Throwing herself into the assignment, she wrote quickly. The words came easily, embarrassingly easy, Laney thought as she covered the page without pausing.

Pastor Bruce pointed to a group of men who held large trash cans. "Okay, folks," he said. "Now we're going to get rid of all that garbage we've been carrying around."

When the usher came to her aisle, Laney reached to throw out her paper. At the same time, Rock discarded his. Laney's paper bounced off the rim and fell on the floor as her hand bumped into Rock's. The usher stepped forward, accidentally kicking Laney's paper through the folding chair and two aisles away.

Rock's hand on her shoulder held Laney in her seat as she rose to retrieve her note. "Don't move off that pen," he said in a low growl.

Frozen in place, Laney mentally cringed at the thought of someone reading her private thoughts and laughing at her mistakes. She twisted in the chair, accidentally clicking the pen. The music started up again, and Laney hunched deeper into the seat with a sigh. Finally the service ended. Rock pulled her arm. "Let's get coffee."

Laney nodded, smiling to herself because it wasn't the coffee Rock wanted. He liked to stand by the gourmet coffee table and compliment women. Demographic research had shown that winning the female vote was the key to election in Sutton County. Rock had political ambitions. "You go ahead," Laney said. "I'll be a few minutes behind you."

As soon as the church cleared a bit, Laney planned to spend the next few minutes on her knees, and it wouldn't be in prayer. She'd be looking for her note, a plan she knew Rock would thwart if he learned of it.

Laney waited until the church had nearly emptied then began looking for her assignment. Two rows behind her she spotted a crumpled piece of yellow paper half-hidden in a discarded service program. With a sigh of relief, Laney stuck the paper into her purse.

She didn't give the piece of paper another thought until later that evening when she decided to remove the

Cinderella pen from her purse. Her fingers found the assignment she'd completed in church earlier that morning. Intending to review her past mistakes and pray for the chance to do better in the future, she was astonished to see unfamiliar writing on the page. Somehow she'd retrieved the wrong note!

As Laney read the words on the page, tears streamed down her face. By the time she slipped into bed that night, she had memorized the letter.

She knelt beside her bed, eyes closed, knowing the writer of the note needed help but unsure of what to do. *Lord, we both know my track record isn't very good, but please use me to help this person.*

The tick of her alarm clock filled her ears, emphasizing the otherwise silent apartment. Somewhere else, someone was alone and hurting. Perhaps he or she, too, sat listening to an empty house. There had to be a way to help. When Laney opened her eyes, she saw a newspaper lying on her night table, and an idea formed.

two

A slender young woman walked over, breaking his concentration and stealing his solitude. "Hello," she said, planting herself right in front of his view of the lake.

Detective Ty H. Steele raised his eyebrows. The last place he'd expected to see anybody was in the middle of a hundred acres of undeveloped land. "I must say, I wasn't expecting you," she continued.

Ty fought the urge to look over his shoulder and see if she was addressing someone else. "What do you mean, me?" He frowned at the freckles across her nose and large blue eyes that stared at him intently. He'd come to the pond on Good Faith's land to be alone. He wasn't in the mood for company, much less for putting on the good face that being a candidate for sheriff required.

"I mean, it's good to see you," the woman replied. She drew her hand through her hair. "I'm here to help you."

Pretty but nutty, Ty thought. "Help me?" He shook his head and held up the McDonald's bag. "I haven't needed help eating a burger since I was a year old."

"Not with that," the woman insisted. Her eyes opened wide in exaggerated patience. "You're here, after all."

This she said as if it made perfect logic. He shifted his weight uneasily. "What are you talking about?"

Her straight, golden brown eyebrows lifted. "I'm talking about the classified in the *Daily Destiny*. I addressed it to the person who left his or her assignment in church last week. I found it."

Ty slapped a mosquito and felt the blood smear on his neck. "Assignment in church? What are you talking about?"

"Oh." Her eyes filled with sympathy. "You're embarrassed. Don't worry. I would never tell anyone what I read."

He put his hands on his hips. "I didn't write any note, and I didn't come here to get saved by you."

She chuckled. "If you didn't come because of the note, why are you here?"

"Because I wanted a spot to eat my Quarter Pounder."

"Well, don't you think it's a pretty big coincidence that you show up at the right spot and the right time?"

His stomach rumbled loudly. "Look—I could stay here all day and argue with you, but I'd rather eat my lunch."

"We don't have to argue," the woman agreed. "We can talk while you eat."

The only way to deal with her was to get rid of her. "We can talk on the way to your car."

"Okay. Where do you want to start?" A slight frown of concentration formed on her lips. "How about with the washing machine incident?"

Ty stopped in his tracks. Nobody knew what he'd done to the machine. He hadn't even called a repairman. He'd intended to take it to the dump and get a new one before anyone saw it. Despite fifteen years of police work, Ty found his jaw dropping in amazement. He quickly raised his hand to rub the skin around his mouth to hide his reaction. "How did you know about the washing machine?"

The woman glanced up at him. Her left eyebrow arched. "How do you think I know? I haven't been peeking through your windows, if that's what you're thinking."

"The assignment?"

"Of course."

Ty watched the silver turtle earrings dangle from her ears. On closer inspection, he realized the turtles were smiling. Usually he preferred his women with more conservative, tasteful jewelry. He could fault Anna Mae, his ex-fiancée, for a lot, but she'd had impeccable taste in jewelry.

"What else was in that letter?"

"You know," she said. "Stuff about your relationships, your feelings."

He stopped walking and touched her arm. Turning her to him, he looked long and hard into her eyes. "You've got the wrong man."

"Sure," the woman reassured him cheerfully. "People all over the county take out their grief on their washing machines."

Muttering, Ty picked up the pace. Bright sunlight dappled the rutted ground, and a few birds called from the trees around him. The woods no longer brought him peace. Ty saw an old blue minivan just ahead. He hoped it was hers. "Hasn't anyone ever told you it's dangerous for a woman to meet strangers in the loneliest part of town?"

The woman nodded. "But that's why I chose this place." She turned her head to look at him. "I know what it feels like to be completely alone."

Ty released his breath in frustration. "You shouldn't be out here by yourself." Even to his ears his voice sounded more like a worried parent than a policeman.

"Where God guides, God provides," the woman said serenely.

"Sometimes He needs a little help," Ty said flatly.

She frowned thoughtfully. "And that's exactly what I'm trying to do."

When they reached the minivan, the woman hesitated. She extended her hand. "Don't give up on God, Detective. Believe me—He hasn't forgotten you."

"How did you know I was a detective?" he said.

The woman smiled. "Your campaign posters."

Ty's eyes narrowed. His police instincts kicked in hard. "What's your name?"

The expression on her face froze. Ty, who had spent his lifetime reading faces, saw the look of guilt stamped across it. "Can I see some identification?"

"That won't be necessary," the woman said. "My name is Laney."

"Laney what?"

Hesitating briefly, the woman's chin lifted. "Laney Varner."

Ty's eyes stopped blinking. "G. C. Varner's daughter?"

As in G. C. Varner, sheriff of Sutton County? He studied her with a different view, recalling bits of office gossip. He'd heard she was cute but flaky, did something with animals, and was engaged to Rock Weyeth, the county's district attorney. His gaze fell to the fat diamond perched on her finger.

Laney leaned forward, her expression earnest. "I'll still help you."

"I don't need your help," Ty insisted. He stepped closer to her. "Did your father send you?" His eyes narrowed.

Laney shook her head. "He doesn't know I'm here. When you decide to accept my help, come and find me."

Before he could reply, she ran to her minivan, pulled the door open, and slid inside to crank the engine. Ty winced at the sound of gears grinding. She wasn't much of a driver, he decided, and hoped she was an equally incompetent political spy.

The van disappeared. Ty looked down at the McDonald's bag, but he was no longer interested in the lukewarm burger or watery soda.

He got into his car. Blasts of hot air blew onto his sweaty face as he waited impatiently for the air-conditioning to kick in.

It was a coincidence, nothing more, he told himself. The truth in the note bothered him more than he cared to admit. He reconsidered the possibility she'd been spying on him.

The more he thought about it, the more the idea hit home. If he were being set up, he'd better find out exactly what was going on, because if she went public with that note, he'd look like an idiot, pulverizing washing machines. He would have about as much chance of being elected sheriff of Sutton County as penguins did of colonizing the Sahara Desert.

He knew what he had to do.

three

Laney opened the door to Animal Ark. Before she had stepped fully inside her pet store, a tricolored papillon jumped out of his basket. Like an airplane roaring down a runway, the seven-pound dog gained speed with every step and launched himself into Laney's arms as she knelt to catch him.

"Don't look so happy," Laney warned. "My meeting didn't go so well."

Angel's tongue washed her face, hands, and ears until, smiling, Laney stood. As always, just being in her store soothed her nerves. She moved about the shop, petting the guinea pigs, talking to the parakeets, and watching the goldfish swarm the front of their tank at her approach. All animals, she believed, had the ability to recognize and give love.

Walking over to the reptile cages, she looked at the corn snake's back then frowned at the pair of lovebirds perched above.

Reaching into the glass tank, Laney carefully picked up the snake and carried it to the supply room.

Intending to wash the snake clean, Laney leaned over the sink and reached for the handle. It stuck. As Laney wrestled with the handle, the snake dropped off her neck and disappeared down the open drain.

In reflex she jammed her hand down the drain and grabbed for the snake. To her relief, her fingers closed over the snake's smooth, dry skin. Closing her eyes, she gave silent thanks and shifted her grip.

She opened her eyes and tugged gently on the snake. The snake didn't budge. She tugged again, a little harder, but couldn't lift it. Evidently the three-foot-long corn snake had instinctively curled in fear, and no matter how soothingly she talked, it wouldn't budge. She was simply going to have to wait for the snake to relax enough for her to get it through the drain.

To pass the time, she thought about Rock and the lovely afternoon they had spent wandering the famous Katherine Whiteman Botanical Gardens. They had picnicked beside a pond filled with lily pads and koi that nibbled at the surface. Rock had held her hand, and they had fantasized about their wedding day. She couldn't wait to marry him. Couldn't wait to share her life with someone who loved her as much he did. It was all she had ever wanted, she thought, to be loved. She hoped he hadn't been up all night scratching the massive mosquito bites he'd gotten.

The jingle of the bell on the store door broke Laney's thoughts, and she cried out, "In the back!"

The even click of hard soles on the tile floors told her that her visitor was large, most likely a man. Her heart leapt at the thought that Rock had come to see her, that somehow he had known she needed him.

"Miss Varner?"

Laney's joy turned to shock and disbelief. The voice sounded as if it belonged to Detective Ty Steele, but she dismissed the thought.

"Miss Varner?" the deep voice repeated.

Laney groaned and pulled her arm gently. The snake didn't budge. When she had imagined herself saving someone from terrible grief, it wasn't while clutching a frightened corn snake curled up in her drain.

"Detective Steele?" Laney called. She twisted to face the front of the room. "I'm in the back."

Seconds later the detective's broad shoulders turned sideways as he squeezed his way through the overcrowded supply room.

Angel growled and stationed himself at Laney's feet. Ty took one look at the dog and said, "That's not a dog. It's an ankle biter."

He might have been telling Angel he'd just been awarded fifty pounds of top sirloin by the way the papillon reacted. The dog's tail wagged frantically, and he all but crawled on his belly across the floor to collapse joyfully on top of Ty's shoes.

Great watchdog, Laney thought, mystified by the dog's show of adoration. The only thing he'd ever shown Rock was a set of fangs—small but impressively sharp.

"You came sooner than I thought you would," Laney said, trying to sound as if this were a good thing. "I'm glad you changed your mind."

"I didn't change my mind," Ty corrected. "I came to get the note."

"First, let's talk about it," Laney said, shifting her grip on the snake.

Ty stepped closer, frowning down at her. "I didn't write that note, but I know who did." His mouth curved into a smile that was not one of happiness. "Your father put you up to this, didn't he?"

Laney's chin lifted, and she tightened her grip on the snake. "My father has nothing to do with this," she said with as much dignity as she could manage with her arm down the drain. "All I want to do is help you."

"Give me the note," Ty said. "I'd like to examine it."

"More likely destroy it," Laney said. "And I can't let that happen. Giving you back that note without talking to you would be like passing a bleeding pedestrian by the side of a highway."

Ty made a sound of disgust. "The way you drive, the pedestrian would be lucky if you didn't run him down."

Laney raised her chin. "You can laugh, but the truth isn't funny."

Ty's eyebrows arched as he seemed to consider her words. Stepping forward, he looked down at her arm. "The truth is your arm is stuck, isn't it?"

It wasn't the truth she had been implying, and Laney fought the deflated feeling that spread through her. "Sort of."

"Want me to get your arm out?"

Laney rearranged her position against the sink. She tried to look nonchalant. "It all depends on how squeamish you are." She met his gaze. "I have a snake in my hand."

Ty snorted. "Sure you do."

"I don't lie," Laney declared.

Moving closer to Laney, Ty leaned over and examined her stuck arm. Shifting her weight under his intense scrutiny, Laney strove to appear calm and in control, although she felt anything but that.

He was tall and muscular and seemed to loom over her. Of course he might not have seemed so imposing if she weren't slightly bent over and holding on to the corn snake. It didn't help either that Angel had chosen to station himself fondly at the detective's feet.

Ty rolled up his shirtsleeves. He put his hand around her arm and pulled gently. When this didn't work, he tried to slip his finger into the drain. There wasn't much room, and his effort tickled Laney.

"What's so funny?" Ty asked, still trying to wiggle his finger deeper into the drain.

"You're tickling me," Laney said. "I'm going to drop this snake if you don't stop that."

"Pull your arm up," Ty said, still struggling to get a grip on her wrist.

Laney raised her arm a fraction. She could tell the exact instant Ty's hand went from her arm to the snake. The shock that went through his strong body was so extremely satisfying that she laughed again.

Ty jerked his hand out of the sink. "Is this a setup?" He looked around in anger.

Laney gave an exasperated cry. "You're the most paranoid person I have ever met. You think I deliberately put a snake in the drain in the hopes that you would come to the store and I could frighten you with it?"

Ty wiped his hand on the leg of his pants. "For all I know, you could have been stalking me for weeks, trying to come up with something you could use against me." He crossed his arms on his chest. "I'm pulling ahead in the polls, and your father can't handle it."

"My father is going to beat you just as he's beaten every other opponent for the past eight years," Laney declared. She blew a lock of hair out of her eyes. "Believe me, he isn't worried."

"Oh, he's worried," Ty argued. "I'd say worried enough to resort to anything—forge a note; send me on a wild goose chase."

Laney tried to throw her shoulders back and appear beyond reproach. Instead, a finger's width of hair returned to its spot over her right eye. "Meeting you by the pond was no accident. I want to help you, but you have to have faith in me."

"Faith in you?" Ty asked. "G. C.'s daughter?"

Wounded, Laney turned her head to meet Ty's cool glare. "Just go away if you're going to stand there accusing me of espionage."

He muttered what might have been a concession then moved closer and peered down at the drain. "It's not a poisonous snake, is it?"

"It's a corn snake, completely harmless." Honesty compelled her to add, "Well, occasionally she does bite."

Ty grunted but reached into the sink again. Even with only two fingers touching her, Laney sensed his strength.

If he wanted to, he could probably pull the entire plumbing out of the bottom of the sink.

"Please stop," she said. "You're going to make me drop her."

The pressure on Laney's arm stopped immediately. "Maybe we should turn the water on," Ty said. "Make it slippery."

"You'll drown her," Laney said, horrified. "How would you feel if you were stuck in a drain with water pounding over your head?"

Ty sighed. "I'd feel like a wet snake."

"That's helpful," Laney said. "Really helpful."

"Well, then, how do you feel about your snake free-falling through the pipe and out the drain?"

"Better than drowning her."

Ty knelt to examine the lower part of the sink. "You have a wrench?"

"On the shelf under the aquarium gravel," Laney instructed.

Minutes later Ty had the drain open. "Let her rip."

Laney dropped the snake and straightened with a groan of relief. She rubbed her aching shoulder and peered down at Ty. "Do you have her?"

"Just a second."

"Don't pull her too hard," Laney warned.

Ty reached into the drain. When the snake still wouldn't come out, he tapped the pipe gently with his other hand. "This isn't working," he said and forced his hand deeper into the plastic tube. He grunted, twisted, and grunted again. A moment later, when his hand emerged, an orange colored snake dangled from his fingers. "I believe this belongs to you," he said.

There was a moment of silence between them as Laney took the snake from his hands. "Thanks, Detective Steele," Laney said at last. She looked at him awkwardly, finding it ironic she had sought to help him, but he had rescued her instead.

"I want to see that note," he said at last.

"Why?"

"I want to have it analyzed. Run the prints. Prove who is setting me up."

Laney rolled her eyes. "This is getting silly," she said. "You and I both know you wrote that note. If I give it back to you, you'll only destroy it. You need help, Ty. Let me help you."

"I want the note," Ty demanded.

"I'll give you back your letter if you agree to counseling sessions with Pastor Bruce."

"That'll never happen, even if—"

The bell to the store jingled, interrupting Ty. For a moment they both froze.

"Laney? Are you back there?"

It was Rock. Her heart began skipping beats. How was she going to explain Ty Steele's presence?

She nearly dropped the snake back down the drain. "It's Rock, my fiancé," she whispered to Ty. Her hands went icy cold as her cheeks blazed with heat.

Ty's face stiffened. "Is he part of this setup?"

"There is no setup," Laney whispered. "You have to stop being so paranoid."

"I will when you give me the note."

The footsteps clicked nearer. "Laney? Are you here?"

"I'm in the back," Laney called.

"I'm getting out of here," Ty said.

"Don't leave," Laney pleaded. "Not until we've had a chance to talk some more."

"You want to talk more?" Ty stepped toward the back door. "Meet me at Miguel's restaurant on Friday night at seven o'clock. Bring the note."

Laney wanted to help Ty, but she didn't think meeting him at a restaurant was a good idea, either. She opened her mouth to protest, but he was already halfway out of the store. The door closed behind him so softly she wasn't sure he was gone.

"What are you doing back here, honey?" Rock looked at the corn snake in her hand and the tools on the floor.

"Trying to help a friend," Laney said.

"With a snake?" Rock laughed.

She realized the corn snake was still in her hands. "Yes, well, things didn't quite work out the way I planned."

"With you, Laney, they never do." Rock smiled good-naturedly. He pointed to the sink. "Do we need to call a plumber?"

"Nope," Laney replied. "She's out."

"She's out?" Rock repeated. "You mean she's out, as in the clog is out of the sink?"

"Nope." Laney ignored the hopeful note in his voice. "I

mean the snake is out of the drain. She—"

Rock held up his hands. "I don't want to hear it. Laney, you've got to be more careful." Rock hated whenever any of her animals got loose. "Can you imagine what would have happened if that snake had popped up in someone's bathroom?"

"I don't even want to think about that happening."

Rock nodded. "After we get married, maybe you should stick to selling cute, furry things, like kittens."

Laney knew he'd calm down if she could make him laugh. "But then I wouldn't have a snake if I got a clog in my drain."

Rock chuckled but stepped backward as the snake stretched in his direction. "Silly girl," he said, "don't you know the snake a plumber uses is a tool, not a real snake?"

Laney batted her eyelashes in the way Rock liked. Of course she knew that. "Well," she said, "in my opinion the real thing would work just as well." She walked out of the room to the sound of Rock's booming laugh as if her simplicity charmed him beyond belief.

four

Three days later, Laney drove into the parking lot of Miguel's, an Italian restaurant located in a new strip mall. The entire mall had a Middle Eastern flare. The buildings, bleached white, loomed large and exotic with gold-domed roofs and rounded pillars that pointed torchlike to the sky.

As Laney pulled into the parking lot, she marveled at the sight of stores like Payless Shoes and Compass Bank looking unfamiliar and self-conscious as if they had been caught playing dress-up.

Wanting to protect Rock from any gossip, Laney had briefly considered disguising herself in a sari. But she'd pictured only too well catching the hem in the front door and the subsequent unraveling of the garment.

In the end, she opted for a different sort of disguise. A search through her closet revealed black karate pants and a black knit top. She'd added two inches to her height with a pair of black, chunky sandals. A French braid controlled her long hair, and a large pair of her brother's sunglasses eclipsed her face. When she had walked into her kitchen, Angel had barked from his basket, thus confirming her disguise.

Still, she paused in the parking lot, scanning the cars

25

with the caution of a secret agent preparing to make a drop. She had no need to be nervous, she told herself; she would slip through the parking lot rendered invisible by the virtue of her mission.

The anonymity effect was ruined when she saw the detective standing by the front door to the restaurant. She met his gaze, and her heart beat faster, more than when she simply got nervous.

Please be with me, Lord. Here we go. Laney slammed her car door and stepped forward. A sharp tug nearly jerked her off her feet, and she realized the strap to her purse had caught in the car door.

Embarrassed, she glanced around. The only eyes that seemed interested, however, were Ty Steele's. Their gazes locked a second time. Her stomach clenched, and her heart knocked against her ribs as if thrown there by force.

Searching for courage to see this secret mission through, Laney walked toward him. Her doubts grew as she neared him. He didn't look like a man who had suffered an inconsolable loss or who needed a woman to listen to him or had ever in his life contemplated suicide.

Instead, he resembled a casually dressed action figure at the toy store. It was all too easy to imagine him gripping the steering wheel during a high-speed chase or vaulting chain-link fences in pursuit of criminals or throwing a thug against a wall as he read him his rights.

For a moment, panic filled her at the thought that somehow she was supposed to help this man. She, who had always attracted disaster as successfully as a tall pole drew lightning, somehow had to find the right words to save this poor, unhappy man from himself.

Okay, Lord, Laney prayed. *We both know James Bond I'm not. I can't do this on my own. If I'm supposed to reach out to this person, You'll have to do it through me, because I surely can't do it on my own.*

She pushed the large dark glasses further up her nose and squared her shoulders, trying not to notice that Ty appeared slightly fierce, as if he were determined to dislike her.

Laney greeted him with a smile, which he did not return.

"Let's go inside," he said.

He opened the door for her, and they stepped inside the restaurant. The combination of her sunglasses and the darkness of the restaurant nearly blinded her. A blast of air-conditioning immediately penetrated her black knit top, adding to her discomfort. It didn't help when Ty's hand touched her arm and guided her forward. His hand on her arm felt unfamiliar. She jerked away.

Rock might not be perfect, but he loved her perfectly. Not a day went by when he didn't call her at least three times to remind her of his undying affection. Just the other day he had volunteered to join the greeters' ministry at church. She had been overwhelmed by his willingness to serve others. His humility made him all the more attractive to her.

The hostess, a young Italian woman wearing black silk, led them to the dining area where about twenty round tables sat covered with crisp white tablecloths. She pointed to a table for two flanked by two large palms.

Ty pulled out the seat for Laney, who was in the process of scanning the room for anyone she knew. To her relief, she didn't recognize anyone, although it was hard to tell with the dark glasses.

"Well, here we are," Laney said, settling into the hard-backed wooden chair.

"I think you can take the sunglasses off now," Ty said dryly. His eyes mocked her. "In a minute you'll have a menu to hide behind."

Laney removed the glasses and sat taller in the seat. "It doesn't matter to me who sees us."

It shouldn't matter, but it did, and she knew it. "Anyway," Laney added, "what's important is for us to trust each other."

Their waitress appeared. "Can I get you something to drink?"

Ty looked at Laney. "What will you have?"

"An iced tea, please."

"I'll have the same."

As soon as the waitress left, Ty said, "Let's get this over with. Give me the note."

"In a minute." She shifted in her seat. "As long as we're here, we might as well get to know each other better."

A sound that might have been laughter came from Ty. "Right," he said. "I'm sure we'll be best friends." He leaned forward. "Let's cut to the chase. Are you planning to blackmail me?"

Laney pulled back so hard the chair tilted at an alarming

angle. "Blackmail?" She bit her upper lip nervously. "Oh, no." She shook her head. "I can't believe you thought that."

"If you are," Ty said, "you can forget it. I didn't write that note, and I'm not paying you a cent for it." His lower jaw moved forward and locked in a position that dared Laney to take a swing at him, verbal or otherwise.

Laney shook her head. "If I gave it to you, you'd probably tear it up." She looked at him knowingly. "Tell me about the man in your note." Her brow wrinkled. "You mentioned your brother."

Ty scraped his chair back from the table. His eyes narrowed to razor-sharp slits. "Tell me you haven't been snooping in my personnel file." He raked his hand impatiently through his hair, leaving a small row of hair upright. "If that isn't proof your father is behind all this, I don't know what is."

"You think my father wrote this note and dropped it onto the floor at church knowing I would be the one to find it and decide to help you?" Laney's brows pushed together. "You are so paranoid."

Ty snorted. "Eventually you'll admit you've been spying on me."

"Spying on you?" Laney shook her head. "Cash registers run out of tape, streetlights fizzle, and traffic lanes close in my path. You think my father would send me to spy on you?"

This information seemed to give Ty pause. "I think he would send his mother if he could dig up some dirt on me." A flicker of satisfaction crossed his face. "He's down ten points in the polls."

"You don't want my grandmother on your case," Laney warned and shook her head. "She has a black belt and a temper. She once karate-chopped the kitchen table in half when my brother Richard wouldn't eat his spaghetti." She paused. "But don't worry—she lives in Kentucky."

For a moment Ty's face went blank. Then, as Laney looked more closely, she saw a slight twitch in his cheek and a tremor run through his mouth. He was trying not to smile. A tremendous sense of victory shot through her. If she could make this large, stern man laugh, she could make him talk. If he talked, she was certain she could guide him out of his depression.

"I suppose you have a black belt, as well," he said at last.

Laney nodded, encouraged by the softening of his expression. "Before she moved to Kentucky, Grammie babysat quite a bit." She toyed with her napkin and hesitated. "My mother died when I was six."

"Charming," Ty drawled. "A little Ninja. The killing instinct was honed since age six."

She looked up, surprised at his sarcastic tone. She hadn't expected this reaction, and it stung. "You're not the only one who's suffered a loss." What had she been thinking to share something personal with him? She might as well have stuck her hand into a lion's cage.

She let the silence fall between them as she tried to pretend he hadn't hurt her feelings.

"I'm sorry," Ty said. "Sorry about your mother."

Laney looked up to find him studying her. It might have been the lighting in the restaurant, but she was certain she saw genuine regret in his eyes.

Laney's heart softened toward him. Whatever his faults were, he'd seen in a glance that he'd hurt her.

"It's okay," she said. "You're safe from my killing instincts. I haven't bumped anyone off since I was nine years old and broke Ken's neck."

Ty's expression stiffened. Laney shook her head. "Ken, as in Barbie and Ken. Dolls." She smiled. "When your father is in law enforcement and he raises you, you play dolls a little differently. I'm probably the only girl in Texas whose Barbie recited Miranda rights, handcuffed, then hauled Ken off to jail when he didn't behave."

The waitress returned with their drinks and set them silently on the table. She turned to Ty. "Are you ready to order?"

Laney looked down at her menu, noticing the selections for the first time. "I'll have the pasta primavera."

Ty's eyes scanned the menu. "Spaghetti and meatballs."

When the waitress left, Laney said ever so casually, "Did you play GI Joe with your brother?"

The last remnants of the smile he'd given the waitress faded from his face, leaving his features harsh. She could almost see him draw away from her without moving an inch. "As if you didn't know."

"Know what?"

Ty leaned forward until Laney could see the flecks of gold in his brown eyes. "Just do me a favor when you're playing your election games—leave my brother out of it."

Laney jumped on his words. "I'm not playing games."

"Stop the concerned look, and tell your father you need acting lessons if you're going to be believable."

Laney decided to ignore the comment. She thought hard about the words in the note. He looked at her as if he hated her. This was fine with Laney. At least he was talking. "Something inside you is making you unhappy." She took a deep breath. "You need to let it out. Isn't that why we're here?"

"In one word," Ty stated flatly, "no." His mouth twisted. "I came here to figure out what damage you can do to my campaign."

Laney gritted her teeth. "This isn't about the election. Tell me about your brother." She calmed her voice and tried to think of an appropriate bribe. "I'll give you the note after you tell me about him."

She thought he would refuse. He appeared angry enough to pick her up, chair and all, and carry her out of the restaurant. Yet something deep in his eyes beyond the anger made her hold her ground. It was a flash of a bleakness of spirit, a glimpse of loneliness and vulnerability. The look vanished almost instantly, and she would have missed it altogether if it hadn't been so familiar. It was a look she'd seen in the mirror hundreds of times and banished a hundred times.

Her heart gave a tug of sympathy. "Please," she said. "I want to know."

His hands lay on the table, his knuckles rising in huge balls of bone that seemed both capable of inflicting damage and swollen, as if they themselves hurt.

When he lifted his gaze, his eyes held a trace of defiance. She met his eyes and deliberately put her hands palm up on the table.

"His name was Mickey." He looked up at her, but it was clear his mind was somewhere else. "He died three years ago."

"How?"

"A school shooting. He saved a group of kids in the path of gunfire."

Without thinking, Laney reached across the table and covered Ty's fists with her hands. In less than a second, her fingers were comforting the tablecloth. Ty scowled at her, as if she'd tried to stab his hand with the butter knife. Covertly her fingers ran over her fingernails to test their points. The blunt tips reassured her she hadn't inadvertently jabbed him.

"I'm sorry about your brother," she said.

Ty's eyes darkened. An odd light burned in them, as if he were about to play a trump card. "Can you explain why your God would let that happen to someone?"

Laney shook her head sadly. "No, but I do know He has a purpose for all of us and a plan for our lives." She leaned closer to him. "You have to trust Him."

Ty made a sound of disgust. "I'd prefer less mystery and a little clearer sign."

"A sign?" Laney laughed. "Have you ever spent time with Him? He speaks to hearts. What do you want Him to do, beep you?"

As the words left her mouth, Ty's beeper went off.

Laughing in surprise, Laney watched him try to cover up his shock as he dug the beeper out of his jeans to check the message.

"There's your sign." Laney couldn't keep the smile off her face.

He checked the number on the pager. "I have to make a phone call," he said. "Be right back."

Laney chuckled, for the first time realizing she had been right to come to the restaurant. She envisioned herself gently leading Ty back to the path of happiness, mending his broken heart. Perhaps they would even be friends. She would be the sister he'd never had.

She closed her eyes and leaned back in her seat, soaking up the moment. *Lord, the credit is Yours.* Even if Ty said nothing else the entire evening, the meeting would be a success. With God's help, he would soon be surrounded by the love of God and his church family.

When she opened her eyes, Laney saw a tall, thin woman in a light-blue silk pantsuit entering the room on the arm of slightly bald man. Even in the dim lighting and from a distance, Laney recognized the woman. Her heart exploded into her chest as Tilly Weyeth, her future mother-in-law, paused. Tilly's long nose pointed as accurately as a compass in Laney's direction.

Laney slid lower in the seat until the stiff, white tablecloth touched her chin; then she took the final plunge and slithered over the edge of the seat onto her hands and knees.

She squeezed between two clay pots and peered through

the palm leaves as Mother Tilly and her date, Malcolm Teeters, the president of Southwest Bank, made their way to the smoking section of the restaurant. Further crystallizing her faith in God, she watched them being seated in a booth that faced away from where she and Ty sat.

"Why, Laney, is that you behind the palm tree?"

She recognized the voice, and goose bumps erupted over her flesh. Turning slowly, still in a crouched position, Laney looked up into the amused blue eyes of Gertha Williams, Good Faith's secretary and leader of the women's Bible study group.

"Hello, Mrs. Williams," Laney replied, reaching for her manners in the absolute horror of discovery. "It's good to see you again."

five

Gertha Williams leaned as far forward on her chair as she could without falling. "Are you ill, dear?"

Laney tried to think of an acceptable reason to be squatting behind the palm trees. She opened her mouth, but no words came out.

Gertha leaned even more precariously forward until she teetered so visibly that Laney feared she might crash. "Is Rock with you tonight?" Without waiting for Laney's reply, she added, "He always has such nice things to say to me at the coffee table after service."

"Rock isn't here tonight," Laney said, hoping Gertha would leave it at that.

Now eye level with Laney, Gertha peered through the tropical plant. It took less than a minute for her to recognize Laney's future mother-in-law and her date. Behind their black-rimmed frames, Gertha's eyes fixed on Laney like blue headlights. "Are you spying on your mother-in-law?" Before Laney could answer, she continued in a shocked tone, "I knew you and Tilly weren't close, but I had no idea things had deteriorated to this point."

"I'm not spying on Mrs. Weyeth," Laney whispered.

"Some people are like heavenly sandpaper," Gertha noted wisely, quoting Pastor Bruce without attribution.

"She's been put in your path for a reason. She has a lesson to teach you."

"Teach me?" Laney replied. "She doesn't even like me."

"Have you given her a chance?" She sighed. "Laney, we need to do some praying together."

"I'm not here to spy on Mrs. Weyeth," Laney whispered.

Gertha's chair creaked alarmingly. "Then why are you crouching behind the tropical plants?"

Laney fought the guilty giggle that worked its way up her throat. "I'm here on church business," she finally managed.

"Church business?" Gertha Williams looked puzzled. "I haven't heard of any church business to take place here." She pressed her lips together. "As the church secretary, I would know."

"I'm sorry, but I can't tell you without breaking someone's confidence," Laney said.

Gertha's skin drained of color. She looked positively ill at the thought of something happening within the church that she didn't know anything about. "Is it part of your Pets-n-Prayers ministry?"

"No."

Gertha swallowed. "Is it evangelical?" She spoke the words so softly that Laney practically had to lip-read them. Besides her job as church secretary, Gertha also led the evangelical ministry.

"Sort of," Laney said. "I really can't say more than that."

Gertha's eyes stopped blinking. Her mind probably was racing through its data bank of people who might know about Laney's evangelical mission at Miguel's.

"I'll pray for you," Gertha said. "Just say the word, and the prayer chain begins."

Laney had no choice except to consent gratefully. Besides, the way things were going, she needed all the help she could get. "Thanks very much," she said.

A quick glance confirmed Ty had not returned to their table. Although she knew their business was far from over, she also knew she couldn't stay. Not and keep her business with Ty Steele private. Not only was Gertha watching her every move, but all her future mother-in-law had to do was turn around and see her with Ty Steele.

And so, before Gertha could question her further, she hid her face in an open menu and left the restaurant.

six

On Saturday evening, Laney had dinner at her father's house.

"Sorry I'm late." Laney slid into an empty seat at the dining room table. Angel jumped into her lap and looked hopefully at the chips and dip sitting in generous quantities on the antique mahogany table.

Her father fingered his gray, lariat-type moustache in silent disapproval. He stretched his wiry legs forward, which sent his chair scraping back from the table several inches. Laney recognized another sign of disapproval.

Rock leaned over to peck her cheek. "Hi, honey," he said. He tried to smooth her hair but stopped when Angel growled. "Bad traffic?"

"A few late shoppers."

Laney looked around the room at the group assembled. Her stomach tightened as she took in the sight of all her brothers seated in her father's formal dining room.

Thomas, Laney's youngest brother, sat at the head of the table, tapping the keys of a laptop. As always, his light brown hair lay in perfect alignment on his well-shaped head. His designer suit hugged the physique of a former high school soccer captain.

"I've called this emergency meeting because Dad has

dropped another five points in the polls," Thomas said. He extended a chrome-colored stylus to the computer-generated graph. "As you can read, we've been losing points ever since Ty Steele entered the race." He tapped the wall. "We need to change Dad's image."

The slide changed to an image of Ty Steele. Laney shifted uneasily. Even one dimensional, Ty's presence made her stomach tighten. She supposed this was fair, because he never looked too comfortable around her, either.

Thomas began reciting. "Hero at age nine when he saved his younger brother from drowning. High school valedictorian. Top ten of his class at Emory University. Law degree from the same school. Fifteen years of distinguished police work."

Her dad waved his hand impatiently. "This is old news, Tommy. Get to the point." Against doctor's orders, he scooped up a pile of potato chips and stuffed them into his mouth.

"He's young and has a good heart," Thomas said bluntly. "Two things you don't have."

His father crunched a chip loudly. "I have wisdom and experience."

"That and thirty cents will get you an operator on a pay phone," Thomas said mildly.

The older man slammed his glass on the table. "When I hired your public relations firm, the last thing I expected was insults." He glared at his son. "I want results."

Richard, the oldest brother, stroked his hickory-colored

goatee thoughtfully. "What about that wedding? There must have been something wrong with him for his fiancée to leave him standing at the altar."

"I looked into that," Thomas said. "While he was at the church, his fiancée was at his house loading up the wedding presents. She pretty much cleaned out the house."

"So why can't people see he's an idiot?" Richard asked. "To let someone take advantage of him like that."

Thomas shrugged. "All the world loves a fool for love, especially someone who looks like Steele. If anything it's made him more popular."

Thomas narrowed his eyes at his father. "If you want to win this election, we have to showcase your strengths." A smile lifted the corners of Thomas's well-molded lips. "Luckily I have a plan." All eyes turned toward their youngest brother, who drew out the moment with a long pause.

"Think about it. Steele's a single man, no local family ties. He's a loner." Thomas smiled at his father. "You're a widower, and you've raised five children."

"That's yesterday's news," his father stated flatly.

"And tomorrow's ace in the hole," Thomas said unruffled. "In one week you're going to make a speech at the dedication of the new municipal building. All the community leaders are going to be there."

"Anybody in Destiny who gets a paycheck from the state of Texas will be there," Rock said.

"Right," Thomas agreed. "That's why you need to stand out. People need to be clear that you're a family man." He pointed his stylus triumphantly. "The person to convey that is Laney."

Shocked silence followed. Thomas's smile widened. "Laney is going to be our secret weapon."

A cry went up from around the table.

"You mean our Laney is going to give a speech?" Richard's eyes bulged in disbelief.

"Laney? Are you crazy?" added Laney's brother Joseph, a shorter version of their father. "Don't you remember the school play when a mouse crawled out of her pocket and all the kids ran off the stage screaming?"

"That was a long time ago," Thomas argued. "We need to emphasize that a vote for G. C. Varner is a vote for family values. People will eat it up."

"It's risky," Greg Varner pointed out. "Laney has a great heart, but she's the kind of person who rescues a kitten and gives everyone in the family fleas." Greg shot Laney an apologetic look.

"I agree," Richard said. "I have the flea bites to vouch for it."

"The future of my public relations firm is riding on this election." Thomas cleared his throat loudly. "I wouldn't gamble my business unless I was sure Laney could do it."

Rock raised his glass. "I agree. I propose a toast to the success of Thomas's campaign." He blew a kiss at Laney and winked at Thomas. "What a great way to introduce Laney to the general public."

The eagerness in Rock's eyes told Laney he was thinking about his future political career. He dreamed of becoming the mayor, a vision he shared often and in detail with her. Once, to her embarrassment, they had even stood out on her deck and practiced waving at imaginary people.

Looking around, she felt the familiar tug to show her family she had what it took to be a Varner. Yet she felt obligated to help Ty Steele. She'd found his note. Now she simply couldn't turn her back on him just because the timing wasn't convenient.

"Laney, you're my only girl." Her father spoke quietly, but his voice carried clearly in the silent room. "I know you like to play with the animals at the pet shop, but the plain truth is that I need your help."

There had been times in Laney's life when she thought her father would rather bleed to death than ask for anything, particularly from her. She looked long and hard at the lines on her father's face and frowned at the thinness of his gray hair.

Being a sheriff meant everything to him. Without the job, some essential part of him might die. He wasn't the type to sit home and watch ball games on TV. He had no hobbies, and his friendships grew out of work.

As her glance widened to include her brothers, she saw the open skepticism on their faces. They saw her as their little sister, softhearted and scatterbrained. Here was an opportunity to show how wrong they were.

Thomas cleared his throat, gently prodding her for an answer. Words either to accept or decline clogged her throat.

Beside her, Rock vibrated with excitement. Finally,

unable to contain himself any longer, he shot to his feet, spilling iced tea from his raised glass.

"Of course she'll do it!" Rock cried. "A toast to the star of G. C.'s campaign!"

As everyone toasted Laney's success, Angel heaved a long-suffering sigh. Putting his head on his front paws, the little dog closed his eyes as if to say it was all too much for him.

seven

When Ty Steele left work Monday evening, Laney tailed him in her minivan. Although Angel insisted on hanging his head out the driver's seat window and the engine ran more roughly than usual, she was pretty sure Ty didn't spot her.

She'd planned to follow him home and then continue the discussion that had been interrupted at Miguel's. But when he pulled into the Kroger's supermarket, she parked several rows away and went inside.

Spying from the bakery, Laney watched Ty place an order at the deli. She pictured his solitary dinner—a roast beef sandwich eaten while he stood over the kitchen sink in an empty house where the loudest noise might be the hum of the refrigerator.

Laney knew too much about empty apartments. She'd discovered a long time ago that no matter how comfortable she made her home or how many pillows she placed on the sofa, when she settled down for the night, there always seemed to be a hard lump. The lump, she had come to realize, was loneliness.

Ty added a bag of whole wheat bread to his cart and headed for the produce section. From behind the banana display, she smiled as he picked out a tomato, gently weighing each one in his large hand before he made his choice.

Although he still looked like a tough guy, the sight of him with a fat red tomato in his hand tugged at her heart. It made him seem more of a solitary figure than ever. The words to his note ran through her head, strengthening her resolve to reach out to him.

In the pasta aisle, while Ty selected boxed macaroni and cheese, Laney crouched by the shelves of rice. Although the shelf held nearly every variety of grain, Laney wasn't looking for rice. She was looking for guidance.

She closed her eyes and tried to block out the background music. *Okay, Lord,* she prayed, *here we are, aisle two in Kroger's. I'm not sure whether it's best to jump out from behind the canned soup display or keep tailing him.*

When the wheels of a shopping cart slid to a halt beside her and a large shadow fell over her, Laney had her answer.

"Hello, Laney," Ty said.

He towered over her, a giant of a man who seemed even larger from her crouching position. She flinched at the slash of his mouth that frowned down at her.

"What a coincidence," Laney said in the bright, false voice that was becoming only too familiar to her. She batted her eyelashes and gave her biggest smile.

"Quit the fake smile," Ty stated. He folded his muscular arms across his chest. "You've been following me."

"I know it seems that way," Laney began.

"It seems that way because it's true." He looked down at her with a grim expression. "Not many old blue minivans drag their mufflers around town. I slowed down so you wouldn't lose Angel out the window."

"Anyway," Laney said, "the point is, now that we're both here, it's an excellent time to pick up where we left off in the restaurant."

Ty rolled his eyes and made a sound of disbelief. "What point are you talking about? The one where you crawled out like GI Jane?"

"I'm sorry about that." Laney stood, hoping he wouldn't seem so intimidating from this perspective. "I can explain."

"You don't have to," Ty said. "But you have to stop this." He put his hands on his hips. "You can't stalk me."

"I wasn't stalking you," Laney said. "I was following you."

"Stop following me, spying on me, and anything else that has to do with me."

Laney touched the silver cross that hung at her throat. She ordered herself to breathe more slowly and ignore the loud thump of her heart. "If someone tried to rob this store, would you try to stop him?"

Ty stepped closer to her. The tips of his leather boots nearly brushed the edge of Laney's canvas sneakers. His size and physical presence made it clear she was no match for him. Yet Laney refused to step backward, not even when he pointed his finger at her. "Of course I would."

"Your note is a cry for help. I can't just walk away."

"Yes, you can," Ty said. "You can stay away from me."

"I can't do that." Laney held his gaze. "Not when we still have so much work to do."

A middle-aged woman pushed her grocery cart closer to

them. Instinctively, Laney and Ty pretended to be concentrating fiercely on their shopping. He smiled politely when Laney handed him a bag of brown rice. She accepted the family-sized box of rice mixture he put in her hands.

Smiling sweetly, Laney placed ten pounds of lentils in his cart. Ty frowned. His eyes narrowed until he saw a five-pound box of processed cheese and added it to Laney's cart. He grinned when Laney's nose curled in distaste. Finally the shopper moved away.

"If you don't stop this, you're going to ruin everything," Ty said. He shifted his weight to his other leg. "Don't you know anything about this election?"

"The election has nothing to do with this," Laney said. "I promise I'm not working for my father."

He ran his fingers through his hair. His eyes were full of skepticism. "You want me to believe you're doing this from the goodness of your heart?"

He made it sound like a crime. Laney's chin lifted. "Is that so unthinkable?"

"Yes, especially when you consider that hounding me could potentially affect every child in our county."

"What are you talking about?"

Ty began to tick off reasons on his fingers. "The security systems and procedures in our schools today are outdated. Your father doesn't see upgrading them as a priority." He paused. "I do."

His eyes held the distant look Laney remembered from the restaurant. "Running around spreading rumors about me doesn't help my election chances." He stared hard into her eyes. "For everybody's sake, stay out of this."

Part of her believed him, but Laney silenced the voice. If she walked away now and something happened to Ty, she'd never forgive herself.

"I'd like nothing better," Laney said. "If my father found out about my helping you, he'd disown me." She raised her left hand. "Not to mention what my fiancé would do."

"We agree then that the best thing would be for you to give me the note and pretend we never met."

"It might be the easiest thing," Laney replied, "but not the best thing."

He stepped so close she could see the length and thickness of his black eyelashes.

"I'm beginning to wonder if there really is a note at all," Ty mused. "Maybe I should call your bluff."

"There's a note all right," Laney said, "and it's a cry for help." She tucked a strand of hair behind her ear. "Don't worry. I have the perfect solution."

"You do?"

Laney ignored the sarcasm in his voice. "Absolutely. What you need is a pet."

"A pet?"

Laney wanted to laugh at the look of horror on Ty's face, except that it wasn't funny. "As a matter of fact, yes." She straightened her shoulders. "I happen to be involved in a ministry at the church called Pets-n-Prayers. It's been very effective in helping people."

Ty rubbed the skin on his face hard. "You're kidding, right?"

"About Pets-n-Prayers?" She shook her head. "It's a proven fact that pets lower people's blood pressure and help them cope with stress." She paused significantly. "Not to mention the power of prayer."

"I'm beginning to think I was wrong," Ty said. He raked his hands through his hair. "Nobody set out to destroy me could come up with a plan like this."

Although Laney knew he'd insulted her, she refused to rise to the bait. "You can borrow Angel if you like. He's a certified companion dog."

"Me with a dog?" Ty laughed. "The plants in my house commit suicide, and I'm talking about the plastic variety."

"You need a pet," Laney said firmly. "I own a pet shop."

"I don't need a pet." Ty's voice rose. "I need a restraining order."

"Neither of us wants publicity," Laney pointed out. "There's a simple solution. You come to the shop tomorrow and pick out a pet. I'll give you back your note." She studied the hard set of his mouth. "Is it a deal?" As the silence stretched between them, she added, "You can trust me."

The very edges of Ty's lips lifted. "Trust me," he said. "Those are famous last words, you know."

"You won't regret it," Laney said softly.

"A note for a pet," Ty repeated. He seemed to consider the idea. "Do you have any plastic fish?"

"No," Laney said.

"You will if any fish gets left in my care," Ty said. "But I will come to your shop." His eyebrows drew together. "And the note had better be there."

"It'll be there," Laney said placidly, completely unimpressed with the formidable expression on his face. "Along with my animals." She didn't like to saddle anyone with an unwanted pet, but an animal to love seemed to be just what Ty needed. "Do we have a deal?"

"I'll come to your shop," Ty said, "but we'll see about the pet."

Laney stuck out her hand and gave Ty's fingers a firm shake. "Come anytime tomorrow. I'll be there."

"Don't even think about sending me home with that snake," Ty said. "The one that went down the drain."

He was joking. That meant progress. Her own spirits lifted with the realization that beneath Ty's gruff exterior beat the heart of a soft man. *He doesn't know it yet,* she thought, *but God is working in his heart, giving him back an ability to laugh.*

"Of course not," Laney replied demurely. "I have a baby alligator that would do quite well in your bathtub."

"You're kidding, right?"

"Am I?" Laney's left eyebrow rose in challenge. "Come to the store tomorrow and find out."

eight

Ty didn't know which bothered him more—his failure to retrieve the note or his growing attraction to Laney. Gripping the steering wheel tighter, Ty tailgated the car in front of him shamelessly until it changed lanes. As the traffic predictably slowed, he signaled, changed lanes, and accelerated. If he couldn't stop his thoughts, then maybe he could outrun them.

The car shifted with the promise of untapped power. He scowled as he passed a car with a bumper sticker: "A vote for G. C. Varner is a vote for family values."

Ty didn't need to be a professional politician to know this new campaign strategy was trouble for him. As if he didn't have enough to worry about with the threat of Laney going public with a note he didn't write.

If he only knew what the note said, he wouldn't worry so much about it, he thought, or obsess so much about Laney.

She continuously popped into his thoughts, disturbed his sleep, and distracted his focus. He couldn't think of a worse time to have a woman on his mind or a worse woman to have on his mind.

Here he was on his way to a pet shop. Worst of all, he actually looked forward to seeing her again. Suddenly he heard a muffled popping noise and felt a slight pull on the steering wheel. Rolling down the window he slowed and listened. Ty heard the clink, barely audible but undeniable, coming from the left rear tire. He had a flat.

Muttering, he eased the car to the shoulder of the road. He saw the Destiny High School lot and pulled in.

Wondering what he'd run over, he rolled up the window, radioed in his position to dispatch, and cut the engine.

At this time in the morning, the lot was filled with cars. A quick scan showed him Beemers, Jeeps, Camaros, a Firebird, Explorers, and even the car of his boyhood dreams—a shiny red Mazda RX-7.

Rolling up his sleeves, Ty popped the trunk. As he put the jack under the car, he found his thoughts returning to Laney.

Could she be as innocent as she seemed? Although he'd accused her of bad acting, the truth was that if she were lying, she deserved an Academy Award.

Sticking the jack beneath the car, Ty raised the vehicle off the pavement. It cocked its flat tire at him as if it were an injured hipbone. Ty wiped his face and reached for the lug nuts.

Since Anna Mae had left him at the altar two years ago, Ty hadn't dated much. He hadn't had the energy or desire to get to know someone well enough to start a relationship. The way he saw it, a man either learned from his mistakes or repeated them. He'd learned.

He'd never forget coming home from the wedding and walking into an empty house. While he'd been waiting to make his vows, she'd been making off with the gifts and furniture.

He pulled the flat tire off the car and tipped it onto the hot cement. Wiping the grease off his hands onto a rag, he looked at his fingers. His knuckles were large, the center one slightly crooked. These were the hands of a policeman—cool, steady.

These same hands weren't so steady around Laney Varner. In fact, every time he was near her, he had the urge to hold her hand. More than that, he wanted to curl a strand of her hair around his finger and see if it was as soft as it looked.

He didn't have a category for someone who looked as fragile as a flower yet held a black belt in karate, who seemed to stumble through life yet held out her hand to help others. Namely him. She made him laugh, she made him paranoid, and she made him wish he'd chosen another spot to have his picnic lunch that day. She also made him glad he hadn't.

A small group of students trickled into the parking lot. He watched all six squeeze into a red compact car. Their clothing nearly brought a smile to his lips. The urge faded when he thought of his brother, Mickey, who had been a math teacher.

He wiped his face. Returning his tools to the trunk, he gave into the urge to lift his face to the sun. For a moment, he closed his eyes, savoring the whisper of a breeze that cooled the sweat on his brow. In his mind, he could almost see Mickey leaning up against a tree, grinning at him from behind his sunglasses.

Mickey led him into trouble, urging the release of the laboratory frogs, urging him to cut class and go fishing with him. He also had been a terrific mimic, able to imitate authority figures with ease and wit. Their Sunday school teacher, Mr. Jones, had caught him once. He and Mickey had spent the morning copying Bible verses as a result. Later, on the hill behind the church, they had rolled in the tall sweet grass, laughing until their ribs hurt.

Ty saw his brother in every teacher who walked through the double doors of a school, heard his voice in the dull roar of students moving in the hallway between classes. Mickey always seemed a ghostlike presence hovering at the edge of his sight.

Ty opened his eyes. He knew he wouldn't find his brother at this school or any other. Yet when he looked up to see a hawk circling in the clear blue sky, he couldn't help but imagine Mickey's spirit soaring free, just like the hawk.

If heaven was real, Mickey would be there. Ty wasn't so sure he'd make it there himself. He and God weren't exactly on speaking terms. Hadn't been for quite awhile.

Ty followed the hawk until it soared out of sight. He found himself in a small courtyard. There were five round cement tables with curved benches for sitting. In the center of the area stood a statue of a boy releasing a dove into the air.

Mickey would have looked at the statue and thought up a good prank. He would have dressed the boy in a tuxedo during prom season or put long ears on it for Easter.

Ty considered leaving a note for his brother in the hands of the statue. It was a crazy impulse, yet it seemed right, like putting flowers on a grave. Reaching into his pocket, he pulled out a small notepad. What should he say? He tapped the pencil on the paper. *Say something,* he ordered himself. *You and Mickey used to do this all the time.*

And then he had the awful thought that if Laney could see him now, pencil and notebook in hand, he would never convince her he hadn't written the note she'd found.

He thrust the pad into his back pocket. The pencil slipped from within the pages and landed with a small noise on the ground.

Squatting, Ty reached for the pencil. As his fingers closed around it, deep lines drawn into the gravel caught his attention. On further inspection, it proved to be a series of numbers. Odder and even more disturbing, they appeared within the drawn outline of a bullet. A chill went down his back.

He had a terrible sense of déjà vu. He rubbed his eyes, wondering if fate was playing a cruel joke on him. But when he opened them, the drawing was still there, larger and more unmistakable than ever.

Was history repeating itself? Ty needed to get to the station to try to convince G. C. to take a more aggressive approach to school security. He had no time to go to Laney's shop and retrieve the note. No time for any more cat-and-mouse games with her. This time he wouldn't let anyone down.

nine

Laney cleared the desk in the back room of her store in preparation for Ty's visit.

She neatly arranged a thermos of coffee, a plate of sandwiches, and a variety of pet-care books across the top. Although she was pretty sure a pair of female guinea pigs would be the best pets for Ty, she wanted him to make an informed choice for himself. Thus the reading materials.

She had books on rabbits, mice, gerbils, ferrets, birds, and fish. Ty could sip his coffee and leisurely browse through the books in private. When he was ready, he could call her back to the office, and she'd bring him whatever animal he chose.

Yawning, she checked the display one more time. She'd spent a sleepless night, tossing and turning and wondering why the hands of the clock moved so slowly. As she'd lain there, no matter how hard she tried to sleep, her thoughts had returned to Ty. She wanted to know more about him, to understand what had happened to his brother, and to unravel the mystery of his past.

Sinking onto the seat, she laid her cheek on the desk. She closed her eyes and tried to picture the big detective holding a guinea pig. She nearly laughed. He'd probably hold it as far away from him as possible, as if it were some

57

bomb that might go off any minute.

"You want me to take care of this tail-less rat?" he'd say. Oh, he would fight her every step of the way. But in the end, Laney knew he'd give in. He might look tough on the outside, but she had read his note. His heart was pure gold.

Distantly, as if in a dream, she heard the jingle of the front door and knew he had come. "I'm in the back," she called.

She heard the sound of boxes moving as he maneuvered through the cluttered room.

"Laney?" a man said.

Laney turned. Her eyes widened in shock. In front of her, smiling with determined kindness, was Pastor Bruce Burke.

"Pastor Bruce," Laney managed. "Wow! This is a surprise."

Pastor Bruce bent over, revealing the purple birthmark on the top of his nearly balding head.

"May I sit down?"

Laney motioned to a chair. "Of course."

"You aren't meeting Rock, are you?"

Laney swallowed. She ran her fingers through her hair and wondered why police bothered with lie detector tests when all they had to do was put Pastor Bruce in a room. "Actually I was meeting a friend who is going through a hard time right now."

The smile faded from Pastor Bruce's face. His brow furrowed in concern. "I don't like to pry, but is everything all right with you and Rock?"

Laney blinked. "Of course," she said quickly. "Why would you think otherwise?"

The senior pastor shrugged. "There have been signs," he said.

"Signs?" Laney repeated faintly. "Letting Mother Tilly eat the gerbil food was an accident. She thought it was granola."

The pastor chuckled. "That's a good one," he said. "Gerbil food and granola. I'll have to use it in a sermon sometime."

Laney hugged herself hard. She could imagine her mother-in-law's hair standing on end at the thought.

Pastor Bruce stroked his chin. "You were seen at Miguel's spying on your mother-in-law." He drew a long breath. "And now half the women in our church are praying for you, although no one is quite sure why."

"Oh." She blinked. "I can explain." But could she?

"The minute I graded your premarital exam, I knew there were problems," Pastor Bruce continued.

"Have a cookie," Laney said, because short of confessing everything, she couldn't think of much else to say. She ripped open a bag of carob-chip cookies.

Pastor Bruce broke off a small piece. "I planned to wait until this coming Sunday for your next premarital workshop session, but I'll just tell you right now."

"Tell me what?"

"The premarital exam you and Rock took last week. . ." The pastor absently pushed the books on the table. When he looked up, his round face looked truly apologetic. "You failed."

"We failed?" Laney hadn't known it was possible.

Pastor Bruce nodded sadly. "You scored a perfect zero. In all my years of counseling engaged couples, I've never seen any couple score so low."

What was Pastor Bruce talking about? Everyone who saw them together said they made a perfect couple. Rock was always solicitous, opening doors for her, handing her his coat in chilly rooms. They even looked alike, with fair skin and sun-streaked brown hair.

"You and Rock need to talk about things," Pastor Bruce concluded gravely.

"We talk," Laney said. She heard the defensive note in her voice. "Just yesterday he left me three pounds of candy bars in a basket on my front steps."

Laney didn't add that peanuts gave her a rash or that she never kept chocolate in the store because it could kill Angel if he ate it.

"Obviously you both care a great deal for each other, but you shouldn't go into a marriage knowing so little about one another."

"We may not know all the details about each other's lives," Laney said, "but we know the important stuff." She drew a breath and wiped hair off her face. "I love him."

Pastor Bruce shook his head. "My test is foolproof. Trust me." He reached for another cookie and broke it in half. "Of course, you know I can't perform any wedding until the couple passes my premarital test." He held up his hand before Laney could protest. "I know it sounds like tough love, but believe me, Laney—it's for your own good."

"You won't marry us?" Laney repeated faintly. Rock would pop a vein.

"Not until you pass the test."

"Can we retest?"

Pastor Bruce beamed. "Absolutely," he said. "You should go home tonight and call Rock. Start talking and find out everything you can about each other." Pastor Bruce paused to wag his finger at her. "It's going to be a different test."

Laney wondered how to break the news to Rock. He hated to fail at anything. She remembered last year's Fourth of July family softball game. The score had been tied and the bases loaded with two outs in the ninth inning. Rock had stepped to the plate, then deliberately into the path of her brother's fastball. He'd received an automatic walk to first base, which had pushed home the winning run.

"I'll call Rock right away," Laney promised. "I'm sure the next time we're going to ace this exam."

Pastor Bruce smiled and rose to his feet. "I'm glad I came here today." He brushed cookie crumbs off his peach-colored polo shirt. "I'm sure all these misunderstandings between you and Rock can be worked out."

Laney looked down at her ring, the symbol of Rock's love for her. "Me, too." She remembered how funny it had felt the first days of wearing the diamond and how she wondered if it had been a mistake to accept Rock's proposal.

She was not blind to Rock's faults. He valued outward appearances more than she did. He loved his clothing and his convertible ad nauseam. When he did his eyebrow thing, only extreme self-control kept her from crossing her eyes back at him. Perhaps worst of all, he came with a mother who had every promise in the world of making her life miserable.

Yet it was because of these things, not despite them, that Laney had accepted Rock's proposal. His imperfections gave her the right to be equally imperfect. She'd seen them as two people moving through life in a clumsy sort of manner. Rock was chronically overgroomed. She viewed herself as the family clown, always trying to gain respectability but never quite achieving it.

She'd thought that together they might find a certain grace both currently lacked. And if great passion was missing between them, Laney felt their devotion to each other and a shared love of God would more than make up for it.

Pastor Bruce peered curiously at the plate of sandwiches and the picnic basket. Absently Laney handed him one. Tonight she'd fix Rock a special dinner. They would talk about everything. After tonight they would have no secrets between them, no subject too sensitive to discuss. She would reach for a level of emotional closeness that most couples only dreamed of achieving. She'd even tell him about finding the crumpled note in the church and her failed attempt to help Ty Steele.

"How's the sandwich?" Laney realized Pastor Bruce had been silent for a while. She loved this about him—his absolute faith in the power of reflection.

"Delicious," Pastor Bruce responded. "Although I must admit, cucumber and peanut butter is a most unusual combination."

"It isn't peanut butter," Laney said with satisfaction. "It's hummus. Much healthier."

Pastor Bruce's forehead creased in concern. "Isn't hummus a type of fertilizer?"

Laney laughed. "Not *humus*. *Hummus*. You think I fed you fertilizer?"

Pastor Bruce smiled but placed the remainder of the sandwich on the desk. "Of course not," he managed, then added, "not on purpose anyway."

"I don't find that *hummurous*," Laney said, deliberately mispronouncing the word.

Pastor Bruce tilted his head to the sky and released a blast of laughter. "You make people laugh, Laney. It's a gift." He grasped her forearm with surprising strength. "Don't let anyone tell you otherwise or try to change you."

I just hope Rock feels the same way, Laney thought. If not, she had a sick feeling that all the jokes in the world weren't going to make him think failing a premarital exam was humorous in the least.

ten

The doorbell rang near the end of Laney's shower. She didn't hear the bell but couldn't miss Angel's howls.

Grabbing a towel, she quickly dried herself off and dressed in her favorite denim skirt and a pumpkin-colored T-shirt.

"Rock's early," she told the dog who darted between her feet. Angel growled. "You better get used to hearing that name," Laney warned the dog, "because we're getting married."

The dog reached the front door and began to wag his tail. Laney slid back the deadbolt. "Good boy, Angel. That's a much better attitude."

When she opened the front door, however, Laney stared straight up into the piercing brown eyes of Detective Ty Steele.

Laney blinked in shock. "Ty?"

"Hello, Laney."

Laney watched Angel launch himself at the detective. The papillon rolled on his back and shamelessly begged for attention. Ty sighed as if this were the last thing he wanted but knelt and rubbed the dog's belly.

Angel certainly likes Ty Steele, Laney thought. And the feeling seemed mutual for him. Maybe he should get a dog of his own instead of a guinea pig. Maybe she would let him borrow Angel for a few days.

Straightening, Ty tried to ignore the small dog that stood on his hind feet demanding attention. The detective looked bigger in the doorway, and she had to tilt her chin to look up at him.

She wasn't wearing heels. That was it. That's why he seemed so tall.

"May I come in?"

"This really isn't a good time," Laney replied. She touched her soaking wet hair. Uh-oh. She felt something foamy. Was that shampoo?

"I'll just be a moment. All I want is the note."

"The note," Laney repeated. She frowned. "You were supposed to come to the pet store." With Rock due any moment, Ty couldn't have chosen a worse time.

"Something came up," Ty said. "Something that makes it even more important you and I talk about the note you found."

Wondering what might have happened, Laney pulled the door open wider. Ty walked inside the apartment as Angel raced ahead barking with happiness.

Laney looked around for her purse. The room was so clean it looked vaguely foreign. For her special evening with Rock, she'd wanted everything perfect. Sighing, she put her hands on her hips and tried to remember where her purse might be. She didn't see it, which confirmed in her mind that putting things away only led to trouble in the long run.

Her hair dripped, leaving a big wet patch on the back of her T-shirt. She could only imagine how she must look. Barefoot, no makeup, and a big gob of soap still in her hair.

"The note," Ty Steele repeated.

"Okay, okay," Laney said. "I'm getting it. Stop glaring at me."

"I'm not glaring at you," Ty said. "I have a lot on my mind."

Laney checked behind the couch cushions. If she had more time, she would have explained that women didn't like to be looked at as if they were about to be arrested. No wonder he was so lonely. And then she remembered where she'd put the note.

She put her hand inside the umbrella stand and pulled out her purse. Her hand trembled slightly as she carefully unfolded the worn paper. She smiled a bit wistfully at the odd tug of her heart and wondered if any other words would move her as much.

Sighing, she gave in to the urge to press the note to her heart. Returning to the living room, she saw Ty staring at a photograph of her and Rock in a twin, heart-shaped frame.

"I'll give you the note," Laney said. "But I'm going to ask you to do one last thing for me."

Ty scowled. "It depends."

"Read the note aloud, once."

Ty shrugged and reached out his hand. Reluctantly Laney gave him the yellow paper. Ty cleared his throat and began to read.

MY FOREVER REGRET

Our two hearts beat as one,
But suddenly you were gone.
To see your sweet face
would be my saving grace.
You were my moon, sun, and stars
When I held you in my arms.
I thought you would be mine forever;
From this mistake I'll never recover.
I put my work first and left you alone,
Neglected you shamelessly; your needs went unknown.
You heard me say I loved another.
Didn't you know I spoke of my brother?
You slipped out of my life
And out of my heart took a slice.
Now when I look at the washing machine,
It looks like something obscene.
An instrument of death, a monster to hate,
Not even when I smashed it did my grief abate.
Depression is my companion, aloneness my friend.
Oh, please, someone, tell me how to make it end.

Ty looked up. His mouth twisted in horror. "You think I wrote that? That has to be the most pathetic excuse for a poem I have ever seen." He raked his hands through his hair. "It doesn't even rhyme properly."

"Well, you were in a rush when you wrote it." Laney knew she sounded defensive. She frowned, thinking she had expected a different emotion to surface when he read the poem.

"I'd have to have been on drugs to write that," Ty insisted. He handed her back the paper. "Here. Keep it. Only a completely insane person would think I wrote that." He laughed humorlessly. "Tell your father he's a much better sheriff than poet."

Laney looked at the smile on his face and saw the truth in his eyes. For a moment she clung to the hope that the look was a pose; but when his gaze met hers without flinching, she knew she'd done it again. Her heart sank to her stomach. Her gaze fell to her hands.

"My father didn't write that poem," she said miserably. "And apparently you didn't either."

She stared at her ring. The fat diamond seemed to wink at her as if she were nothing more than a joke. The enormity of her mistake crushed her to the bone.

She'd made an idiot of herself, sneaking around restaurants and even tailing him to the grocery store. How could she think God would choose her to do His work? It was all true—every Calamity 'Lane joke.

She hung her head in her hands. "I'm such an idiot."

"You finally believe me." Ty sighed in relief.

Laney looked at him through tear-filled eyes. "I was so sure I wouldn't mess up things this time."

Ty coughed and looked away. "It was an honest mistake."

"Right," Laney said. "Like anyone else would pick up a note in church and do what I did." She sniffed. "Can you believe I actually thought God was giving me a chance to make up for all the times I've goofed up?"

"I'm sure you meant well."

Laney shook her head. "I'm the last person who should try to help someone else. I'd probably shove someone off the roof trying to save them from jumping."

"You're not so bad," Ty said in the stilted sort of way that told her clearly he was lying. "Besides, they have safety nets for jumpers these days."

She tried to laugh, but the noise sounded more like a sob.

"I was only joking," he said. "I'd trust you to save me if I needed it."

She looked up, and her hands fell away from her face. "You would?" She wasn't sure she believed him, but she could at least hope he meant it.

"Sure," Ty replied. He shifted an inch farther from her on the sofa. She watched his gaze go to the door. "Nobody's perfect all the time," he added.

"But I'm imperfect all the time." Laney nodded. "It's the truth."

"It's not the truth," Ty replied. "Not just anyone is willing to help a stranger." For the first time she heard sincerity in his voice. "Believe me—most people are interested only in themselves."

Laney's heart began to beat harder, as if the sadness had been a weight that had been removed. Right now she felt closer to him than she ever had to any other person on earth.

"You're not just interested in yourself, either," she said. "I remember what you said about helping make schools safer when we were at the grocery store."

She couldn't seem to look away from him. He was gazing at her differently, as if he saw something new and good about her.

When his gaze dropped to her hands, she realized she'd been twisting her engagement ring around and around. Of course she would have to tell Rock what had happened. He'd be horrified, but she hoped he would understand.

"I probably should go," Ty said.

Laney looked up, feeling strangely bereft yet finding she couldn't think of anything to say to him.

"You might want to wash that shampoo out of your hair before your company arrives," Ty suggested. His mouth lifted at the corner, and she could see he was trying to coax a smile out of her.

Her cheeks grew hot. "Yeah, well, sorry for all the inconvenience I've put you through." She stood and walked toward the door. "Good luck with the sheriff's race."

"Don't set up any more meetings by that church pond," Ty warned her. "It's too isolated." He paused in the open door. "Take care of yourself, Laney." And then he was gone.

eleven

Laney rinsed off the gob of shampoo with the hose in the sink. But before she had time to dry her hair or change into a dressier outfit, the doorbell rang. Hair dryer in hand, she glanced at the bathroom mirror and groaned. This wasn't the way she'd pictured meeting Rock at the door for their special dinner.

The doorbell rang again, followed by knocking. Angel barked and tugged at the hem of her skirt. Putting down the dryer, Laney combed her damp hair behind her ears. She took a deep breath for courage and headed for the front door.

She'd barely entered the living room when she heard a voice call from the other side of the door. "Laney, are you in there?"

She froze. Angel growled. She and the dog exchanged glances. She knew they were thinking the same thing. The voice on the other side of the door belonged to none other than Mother Tilly.

Trying to hide her dismay at the thought of finding her future mother-in-law at her front door when she looked far from her best, Laney swung open the door.

"Laney, we thought you might be dead on the floor," Tilly Weyeth said, with Rock standing beside her.

Angel charged through the open space and circled the visitors at full speed. He dodged Tilly's foot as she aimed a kick in his direction.

"Sorry, but I was still getting ready," Laney said.

"That much is obvious." Mother Tilly frowned. As if the sight of her future daughter-in-law's wet hair and bare feet was nearly unbearable, she focused her gaze over Laney's left shoulder. "Rock said we should come at seven o'clock."

Laney forced herself not to look at her watch, though she was pretty sure it wasn't that time yet. "Well, come on in!"

Rock kissed her cheek as he passed her. She caught a whiff of his ginseng-scented aftershave. It smelled as smooth as his freshly shaven cheek against hers. She looked at the shopping bag in his hands. "What's that?"

"Dinner," Mother Tilly said, as if she were surprised Laney should have to ask. "I made beef bourguignon, salad, rolls, and a Dutch crumb apple pie for dessert."

Laney's gaze found Rock's. This was supposed to be their evening. His mother wasn't invited, and neither was her beef bourguignon.

What had happened to the quiet evening she'd planned for them together? Her dinner, vegetarian chili, simmered on the stove; her corn bread heated in the oven; and chocolate ice cream waited in the freezer.

Rock's smile materialized on his face with the grace of a magician pulling a rabbit from his hat. Laney recognized the expression as one he used to pass off an especially farfetched compliment at the donut table at church. "I invited Mother to join us for dinner tonight."

Rock rearranged a clump of Laney's wet hair to the correct side of her part. "I knew you wouldn't mind."

"Oh," Laney said. In fact, she did mind. She minded a lot. Her mouth opened and then closed. She would forgive Rock for his insensitivity and hoped that later, when he learned about what happened with Ty Steele, he'd forgive her.

"When Rock told me about that little mishap with the pastor, I knew I had to come right over and help," Mother Tilly said. She took the shopping bag from her son's arms. "I brought some things to help you ace that premarital test," she said. "Rock can bring the rest of the bags from the car after dinner."

"Rest of the bags?" Laney whispered.

"Mother brought her cookbooks, volumes one through five." Rock blew a kiss at his mother. "She's marked all my favorite recipes for you."

"And I'm going to explain how to make each and every one," his mother promised. Her gaze continued to rest lovingly on her son. "And I'll make Laney copies so she can start her own notebook of Rock's favorite foods."

"Isn't she great?" Rock said enthusiastically as he spontaneously threw an arm around his mother's shoulder. "And that's not the only surprise Mother has for you tonight." He winked at Laney. "But I don't want to give everything away at once."

"Now you'll have to excuse me," his mother said, slipping out from under her son's arm and smiling broadly at him. "I want to warm up dinner."

Tilly's black silk skirt swished around her legs as she

crossed the small apartment to the kitchen.

Laney stared hard at Rock, wondering how he could stand there looking so satisfied. Every inch of her shrank at the prospect of his mother instructing her on how to please Rock.

"We were supposed to talk to each other tonight," she whispered. She pointed to the dining room table where she had placed a yellow tablecloth and topped it with sky blue plates. "We need time alone together to discuss things."

"I had a better idea," Rock said. "After you told me about failing the premarital, I knew I had to do something." He paused. "My mother is our secret weapon. I'll eat my shirt if Pastor Bruce comes up with something about me on the exam that she won't cover tonight." He stroked his chin thoughtfully. "Maybe you should take notes."

"Are you serious, Rock?" Laney asked. Her voice rose. "Why don't we just have your mother stand outside the window with cue cards when we take the test?"

"Because we don't know exactly what questions are going to be on the exam," Rock replied patiently.

"Rock." Laney lowered her voice, keenly aware of his mother in the kitchen. "I want to know the deep stuff about you. The things you never told anyone else. Your fears, your dreams, those kinds of things."

Rock cocked his head at her as if unsure what had upset her. He gave her a small coaxing smile. "That stuff won't be on the exam," he said. "Mother can tell you everything you need to know."

" 'Mother can tell you everything you need to know,' " Laney repeated in frustration, imitating Rock's voice more closely than she'd known possible and drawing back when she saw the look of shock on Rock's face.

"Mother," Rock called loudly, "someone out here isn't in a very cheerful mood tonight." He raised his eyebrows as he always did when he was trying to convey a show of patience above and beyond human capability. "You'd better come right out here and give her the present."

"I don't want a present," Laney protested. "And if I'm not cheerful," she said, "it's because—"

Laney's words broke off as Tilly walked into the room and, without sparing Laney a glance, reached her son's side. Her eyes gleamed with the pleasure of teaming with her only son.

"With that wet hair, she's probably freezing," Tilly explained, "or embarrassed because she wasn't ready for us." She flashed her son a smile that said she loved him despite his poor taste in women.

Frowning, Laney dragged her hand through her wet hair. She resisted with effort the urge to protest she was neither cold nor embarrassed and that Tilly could speak directly to her.

Tilly opened her purse and pulled out a large black velvet jewelry case. Laney couldn't explain the sudden dread that shot through her at the sight of the velvet case.

"It's the Weyeth lavaliere," Tilly said lovingly, handing the box to Rock. "Every bride in the Weyeth family wears the necklace at her wedding." Her fingers touched the gold chain as if remembering long ago wearing the lavaliere at her own wedding.

Rock lifted the necklace from the box reverently. He let it dangle from his fingers. "Isn't it beautiful?"

Beautiful wasn't the word that came to mind. Tacky, gaudy, and downright ugly described it better. Embedded in a patchwork of semiprecious stones was a series of small diamond chips that formed the letter W. It was the size of a silver dollar, and more than anything it looked to Laney like an oversized dog tag.

"I'm speechless," Laney said at last.

Rock and Tilly let out their breath simultaneously and exchanged looks. "Put it on now," Rock said. "I've been looking forward to seeing this on you all day." He smiled with boyish excitement. "You can't imagine how hard it's been keeping it a secret from you."

Laney swallowed. "I imagine it was." And then because Rock was looking at her as if he had found pirate gold to lay at her feet, she added, "It really is incredible."

Rock raised the necklace. Tilly's hand slapped it down immediately. "She shouldn't put it on with wet hair." Her lips puckered. "And it would go better with a"—she paused—"a different outfit."

Laney sighed with relief, despite the insult to her choice of clothing. Rock frowned thoughtfully. "You're quite right, Mother." His moustache drooped to reflect his disappointment.

"I'm sure Laney has lots of suitable outfits in her closet," Mother Tilly continued. "We'll just go and pick one out right now. How's that, Rock?"

"Great idea," Rock said, brightening immediately.

"No, really," Laney said. "The necklace deserves nicer than what I have. Plus my hair is wet. Another time probably would be better."

"No, no, no," Mother Tilly said. She turned in the direction of Laney's bedroom. "Nothing like the present for our present." She smiled at her words. "Come on, dear," she directed to Laney's left ear.

As Tilly marched off to the bedroom, Laney tried to remind herself that, as Pastor Bruce said, some people were like heavenly sandpaper. She wondered what lesson Mother Tilly had to offer and what rough edges of her personality would be made smooth by her future mother-in-law. Ordering herself to hold on to her temper, Laney stepped inside her bedroom.

twelve

Mother Tilly headed straight for Laney's closet. Pulling the sliding door open, she gasped. "Is there any order to this closet at all?" She clucked her tongue as she sorted through the skirts and tops. "I group by designer," she explained. "It's a real time-saver. When Rock runs for mayor, you'll see how this helps."

Laney nodded, although she thought the day she alphabetized her clothes would be the day she checked herself into a mental hospital. Still she didn't protest as Tilly plowed steadily through her closet.

The room, small to begin with, felt even tinier with Mother Tilly in it. Feeling as if she couldn't breath, Laney swung open the sliding glass doors and stepped outside to the deck. The night air, though nearly the same temperature as inside, immediately seemed fresher, and she felt some of the tightness in her chest ease. How would she tell Rock the secrets of her heart with his mother there?

"Don't you have any black silk?" Mother Tilly called from the closet.

"No, Mother Tilly," she replied. In fact, she didn't own many dressy clothes at all. She loved gauzy, light skirts of bright colors, knit tops, and oversized cotton shirts. She fervently hoped Tilly wouldn't uncover one of the bridesmaid's dresses she had stuffed in the back of her closet.

She didn't want to go back inside her apartment. Not with Mother Tilly finding fault with every garment of clothing she owned. Strangely, she didn't feel like spending time with Rock either. She felt like staring up at the night sky and trying to figure out why her life suddenly felt so out of control.

"I think I've found something."

Laney cringed. She had the awful feeling Mother Tilly had just discovered the crimson taffeta dress she'd worn at Richard's wedding.

Her fears were confirmed the minute she stepped back into the bedroom. "Here, dear," Tilly said. "This will go well with the lavaliere."

Laney shook her head. "I appreciate your help, Mother Tilly, but I think I'll just keep what I have on."

Holding the dress up to her, Tilly smiled coaxingly. "Come on, dear. Rock will be so pleased to see you looking so nice."

Shaking her head, Laney took a step backward. "I don't think so. Maybe another time."

"Laney, as Rock's wife, you're going to have to get used to wearing formal clothing. Some day he could be the mayor, you know, or even a senator."

"When the time comes," Laney said, "I'll deal with it." She was having trouble breathing again and glanced longingly at the open sliders that led to her deck.

"Humor me, Laney," Mother Tilly pressed. "Wear the dress."

Laney felt the color drain from her face. First it would be wear this dress, and then it would be cut her hair and change her makeup. She saw her life as a series of compromises she would make until she was completely unrecognizable to herself.

"I'm not wearing the dress," Laney heard herself say loudly. "And you can't make me."

Tilly wiggled her eyebrows at her the way Rock did when she displeased him. And as usual it sent a rush of irritation through her. As if she were standing outside her body, Laney watched herself take the dress from Tilly and rip it down the middle.

"I'm not wearing the dress."

Eyes bulging, Mother Tilly clutched the Weyeth lavaliere to her breast. A small sound of distress squeezed through her throat like air released from the pinched neck of a balloon.

Suddenly there was a knock on the door. "You girls okay in there?" Rock's voice rang with worry.

"We're fine," Laney shouted back.

"You sure?" Rock prodded. "I heard something tear." There was a slight hesitancy, and then Rock chuckled. "Mother, you okay?"

"I'm fine," Tilly called back in a strained voice. Her gaze fixed on the dress, which lay on the floor in a torn heap.

"Perhaps you were right, dear," she said. "Trying out the Weyeth lavaliere is best left for another day."

Laney smoothed her damp hair. What had gotten into her? Already she regretted her action. "Good idea, Mother

Tilly," she said. "I'm sorry. I don't know what got into me."

"I'd better go check my beef bourguignon," Tilly said. "Rock will be disappointed if it burns. It's his favorite, you know."

৯

Afterward Laney couldn't quite remember how she had gotten through the evening. Trying to make up for her inexplicably bad behavior, she'd done her best to follow Tilly's instructions. Her nerves were jumpy, though, and no matter how hard she tried, she couldn't concentrate. She forgot to put the lid on the blender, and as a result, Rock's fruit smoothie ended up on her ceiling.

When the door had finally closed behind Rock and Mother Tilly, she breathed a sigh of relief and stepped out on her deck.

To her surprise, she saw Ty Steele sitting on a bench in the sheltered garden just beyond the deck. She walked to the railing and put her hands on her hips. "What are you doing there?"

"Waiting for them to leave," Ty said. "I didn't think you'd appreciate another unwanted guest for dinner."

Bracing herself against the railing, Laney crossed her arms. "I thought you left hours ago."

Ty shrugged. "I would have, except I left my car keys on your coffee table."

"You mean you've been here the entire evening?"

"Just some of it. I took a walk around the block after you ripped up the dress. Good going, by the way."

He'd overheard her fight with Tilly? Laney felt her

cheeks heat up. Only too well she remembered leaving the sliding door to the deck open.

"I'll go get your keys," she said.

When she returned, he had stepped out from under the trees and was looking up at the moon. It reminded her of how she had gazed up at it earlier. She wondered if he, too, recognized that something was wrong with his life but didn't quite know how to fix it. He finally turned around.

"Sorry you had to wait so long for these," she said and handed him the keys.

"No, I'm sorry for you," Ty said.

"For me?"

"They were really on your case for failing that premarital exam. You should have told them it works both ways. He has to get to know your life as much as you have to get to know his."

Laney sighed. "The least you could have done was put your fingers in your ears. That was supposed to be a private conversation."

"Just you, Rock, and Mother Tilly," Ty said agreeably. "You all make a great couple."

Laney bristled at his words, angry because he was right, frustrated because he understood something Rock hadn't. "She was just trying to help, you know."

"How do you stand it?" Ty asked suddenly. "They talk to you as if you are a total moron."

"Rock adores me," she said.

"Doesn't it frighten you that you have to count the

number of times you stir the coffee? 'Steady hand, girl,' "
Ty parroted imperfectly but effectively.

Laney waved her hand. "It's just for the test," she
replied.

"No, it isn't," Ty warned. "They're trying to turn you
into a copy of his mother, and you don't see it."

"That isn't true," Laney protested.

"What you cook, how you arrange your clothes in the
closet, what you wear. . ." Ty shook his head.

"This isn't any of your business, is it?" She crossed her
arms on her chest.

Ty's gaze fixed on hers. He didn't seem able to stop.
"And that necklace she wants you to wear. The plug in my
bathtub is more attractive."

"That's a family heirloom," Laney snapped. "A symbol
of love."

"Symbol of love?" Ty's smile had a fiendish air. "More
like a symbol of service—a gold ball and chain to hang
around your neck."

"What right do you have to talk about my relationship?"
Laney's words flew off her tongue like arrows off a bow.
"What do you know about love?"

Ty glared at her. "I know what love isn't. It isn't about
lessons in making coffee or quizzes about favorite books
and movies."

His face, shadowed, looked even harsher than usual,
almost in controlled anger. She saw the prominence of his
facial bones, the lines fanning from his eyes, the scar near
his hairline.

"Love isn't two people in the same room with nothing to talk about. Love isn't what someone can give you or what you can get from them."

She couldn't tell the exact moment when the anger in his eyes turned into something else. Only that it had. She looked away, not wanting to see that things had changed for him.

Laney took a step backward as he approached the deck, his hand on the railing, as if he would climb over it. She saw his purpose in the intensity of his gaze.

Her hands fumbled along the railing then closed around a plastic watering can. In one swift motion she emptied it down the front of his shirt.

They both stood, speechless, watching as water dripped onto the ground. Ty squeezed water out of his shirt.

"I've been punched, kicked, and shot at, but never watered down." He shook his head as if in wonder. "You're something, you know that, Laney?"

Laney didn't deserve his admiration. She was more than glad that Ty Steele no longer needed her help. He needed dry clothes, perhaps, but not her.

She, on the other hand, needed a lot of help. *Heavenly Father,* Laney prayed, *somehow I misread signals and have been trying to help the wrong person. Please forgive me for following Ty Steele and now for ruining his clothing. Please give me a new plan, Lord, and another chance to make things right.*

thirteen

Laney's new plan involved a stakeout. On Sunday morning at church, she watched the gymnasium fill. People she knew by sight but not by name smiled at her. She waved back, wondering if they had seen Rock in the parking lot greeting people.

Laney sat straighter in her seat, filled with a quiet pride in the knowledge that Rock could be counted on to do a job well. He gave new meaning to the word *dependability*.

Music soared through the gymnasium, announcing the beginning of the service. The last stragglers hurried to their seats, and a couple settled themselves into the very seats Laney had been watching.

She couldn't believe her eyes when she recognized Terry and June Whitley, friends since high school. Although she and June had gotten a bit out of touch the last few years, Laney still counted June as one of her closest friends. It dismayed her to think her friend might have been the one to have written that sad note. At the same time, she wouldn't repeat her last mistake. Before she confronted June about the note, she would do her best to find evidence that June or her husband had written it.

Two days later she found herself on June's doorstep.

"I'm so glad you suggested getting together this evening,"

June said. She held the door to her house wider. "And you brought Angel." She bent to greet the dog. "How's my best buddy?"

"He's fine," Laney said. "Hope you don't mind that I brought him."

"Don't even worry," June replied. "It'll be great to spend time with both of you." She smiled in apology. "Between the business and the kids and Terry, I don't seem to have a minute to call my own."

"I know what you mean," Laney said.

Laney walked past her into the restored Victorian that served both as home and business. Angel trotted happily inside, checking out the sights and smells.

June and Terry lived on the second floor. The first floor had been converted into a full-service beauty salon.

"I hope you know," June continued as Laney settled herself onto the couch, "that I'm here for you. You can call me anytime."

Here for her? Laney frowned. She was supposed to be here for June. Not that June appeared to need help. Her friend looked wonderful. The new color and short, choppy cut framed her round face perfectly.

Gazing into the mirror on the wall, she saw that she, on the other hand, had dark circles beneath her eyes and cheeks as pale as the moon. She looked as if she hadn't slept in days, which was the truth.

"When I saw you in church," Laney said, "I knew we had to talk."

"Is it about Rock?" June fingered a spike of hair around

her ear and sighed in a sympathetic sort of way. "Nobody tells you how stressful an engagement can be." She took Laney's cold hands in her own.

Laney had the sudden urge to confess the real reason for her visit. Before she could say anything, however, the ceiling rumbled with the force of running feet, excited shouts, and giggles.

"If you want to talk stress, though, try dealing with five-year-old twin boys. Some days I think I'm going crazy." She shook her head. "Plus we've been without a washing machine for two weeks. Talk about wanting to cry!"

"What happened to it?" Laney asked, her mind jumping back to the reference to a washing machine in the note she'd found.

June shrugged. "I'm about ready to take a sledge hammer to it." She sighed. "It flooded our laundry room, and now it's sitting by the garbage cans. Terry thinks he can fix it." She shook her head. "You should see the list I have of things that need fixing—everything from the doorbell to the toaster oven."

Laney leaned forward. "I want to know all that's going on with you."

June chewed her lower lip thoughtfully. "You know what? We'll give each other a complete beauty treatment. I'm talking facials, deep-conditioning shampoo, even a body wrap. Then we'll head up to the guest room where no one will bother us, and we'll stay up all night talking like we used to. How's that?"

Angel barked in excitement. June patted his soft nose

and ran her hands over his large, winged-looking ears. "We'll do you, too, Angel. Put bows on you."

Angel grinned. Laney knew he liked nothing more than being in the center of the action. "Sounds like a plan," she said.

"I'm closing the shop," June declared. "Terry has the kids. The evening is ours. Let's start with our hair and work down." She eyed Laney professionally. "How do you feel about blond highlights?"

Laney sighed and prepared for the worst.

Hours later, with her hair in multiple tinfoil spikes, her face plastered with a green cream that hardened into a glue-like cast over her face, and her nails painted hot pink, Laney still hadn't learned a thing about her friend or her washing machine.

"Go put your bathing suit on." June pointed to the bathroom. "We'll do a seaweed wrap next."

When Laney returned minutes later, June stood in front of a bathtub filled with thick green mud. "You go first," June urged. "This is so good for your skin. Believe me. You'll get that radiant look everyone expects brides to have."

Laney looked at the tub doubtfully. Even Angel, after peering over the rim, retreated. But she couldn't disappoint her friend, so she eased into the depths of what she thought of as a dark lagoon.

The seaweed smelled surprisingly of eucalyptus, and Laney leaned further back, letting the scent work through her body. Muscles she hadn't known were tense slowly unknotted in the warm, silky mud.

"Put this on your eyes," June said, handing Laney a black gel mask. "It'll take away those circles."

Laney tied the ends of the mask. She felt like a combination of the Lone Ranger and the Creature from the Black Lagoon. Not so much, however, that she forgot the purpose of her visit. "So marriage is good then," she said.

June perched on the edge of the tub. "Wow! You are having doubts about marrying Rock."

"Mom!" Two boyish voices rang clearly through the house. June looked at Laney with a combination of pleasure and impatience.

"I have to tuck them in," she said, smiling. "They won't go to sleep otherwise." She stood. "Be right back."

As soon as June disappeared, Laney climbed out of the bathtub and toweled off. *Okay, Lord,* she thought. *I hope You're enjoying this.* She slipped into her sweat suit and headed out the back door to check the state of the broken washing machine.

The back door closed with an ominous click, and even before Laney put her hand on the knob, she knew it had locked behind her. Blinking as her eyes adjusted to the darkness, Laney stared at the locked door. She wanted to bang her head against it. Why did it always seem as if Murphy's Law had been written just for her?

Trying not to worry about how she would get back into the house, Laney put this setback behind her and followed the concrete stepping-stones to the back of the house. She stubbed her toe and would have gotten a nasty scratch on a protruding branch if not for the thick facial mask.

Near the back fence an oversized garbage can sat next to a forlorn-looking washing machine. Laney stepped closer. As far as she could tell, it didn't have a scratch. When she opened the lid, the insides looked like those of any other washing machine.

Frowning, Laney closed the lid. June had been exaggerating. No one had smashed the washing machine during a grief-stricken rampage. She could cross June and Terry off her list. Now the problem remained. How could she get back into the house?

She remembered the doorbell didn't work. At the risk of summoning the neighbors, Laney didn't want to pound on the door or shout. The twenty-four-hour gas station and convenience store seemed a reasonable solution. She could telephone June from a pay phone.

She was thankful plenty of loose change had found its way to the floor of her minivan. She was also glad she'd left it unlocked. She retrieved enough money to call and headed toward the gas station. She drew the hood of her sweatshirt over her head so the aluminum foil wouldn't reflect the streetlights. The seaweed wrap had begun to dry and itched horribly. Her stubbed toe stung, and she wondered what color her hair was turning under the foil.

Please don't let anyone see me, Laney prayed. She walked more quickly. When she reached the gas station, she peered through a corner of the window to make sure no one was inside.

Satisfied with the emptiness of the convenience store,

she swung the door open and walked in. Her bare feet slapped on the cold, polished floor as she crossed to the pay phone. She'd nearly reached her destination when the clerk turned and saw her.

For a moment they both froze. They locked gazes, each mirroring the same horrified expression. The clerk, a heavyset man with a ruddy complexion, recovered first. "Take whatever you want—just please, don't hurt me."

"I'm not robbing your store," Laney said. "Look," she said. "No gun." She held out her arms, which trailed particles of the green seaweed wrap.

"Angel of death," the frightened clerk gasped as he hit the silent alarm and then fainted.

fourteen

Ty Steele drew his pistol and threw open the door to the Eat and Go. He spotted the suspect immediately, a cloaked dark figure crouching over the prone body of the clerk.

"Police!" he yelled, scanning the store for other perpetrators and gripping his pistol with both hands. "Freeze," he ordered. "Drop your weapon and move away from the man."

The suspect eased backward. Ty couldn't tell if he had a weapon under the black hooded sweat suit or not. "Put your hands up," Ty said, moving closer, simultaneously assessing danger and injury to the prone clerk.

"Okay," he told the suspect. "Turn around slowly with your hands in the air."

With one hand steady on his gun, Ty reached for his handcuffs. His fingers froze as the suspect's face became visible. His eyes widened then narrowed. It had to be some sort of mistake. The suspect had green skin. And if that wasn't bad enough, it looked like Laney Varner. It couldn't be, could it? "Is that you, Laney?"

The suspect nodded and slowly pulled the hood off her head. Ty felt his jaw drop. "You're green."

"I know it," Laney said.

"And you're wearing tinfoil in your hair."

"It's a beauty treatment," Laney snapped. "Don't stand

there. You have to do something. I can't get Mr. Zoowalsky
to open his eyes."

Beauty treatment? Only if she were a Martian. Ty knelt
beside the clerk and put his fingers on the man's wrist.
He felt a strong, steady pulse and watched the even rise
and fall of the man's chest. He checked for other injuries
and found none.

Unable to resist, he shot Laney a sideways glance.
"What happened?" he asked. "Did your spaceship run out
of gas?"

Laney groaned. "I got locked out of my friend's house. I
just wanted to use the pay phone." She pointed to the wall
behind them. "When the clerk saw me, he fainted."

Ty bent over the inert man. "Open your eyes, Mr.
Zoowalsky. You're okay."

"He thinks I'm an angel of death," Laney said. Ty heard
the misery in her voice and fought the urge to smile.

"He's going to be fine. You just scared him a bit—that's
all." Ty paused. "We'll get him checked out, but my guess
is that he's playing possum."

"I'm so sorry, Mr. Zoowalsky," Laney said. "I didn't
mean to scare you. Please open your eyes."

Mr. Zoowalsky shook his head.

Ty's eyes twinkled as his gaze swept over Laney's face.
"You want to tell me how you happened to get locked out
of your friend's house?"

"I was checking out a lead," Laney admitted. "I haven't
given up looking for the person who left that note behind
in church."

He stroked his chin. "You'd better find that writer fast before you kill off half the town."

Laney glared at him. "Very funny."

Ty smiled. He couldn't help himself. She looked cute in the funny makeup. No real harm had been caused, and he would do his best to help put things right for her. "Why don't you go get cleaned up?"

Laney sighed and fingered the tinfoil in her hair, managing despite the Martian appearance to seem very human and vulnerable.

Ty reached over and squeezed her hand. "You should go," he urged. "Go back to your friend's house and get cleaned up. I'll handle this. My backup will be here soon."

Laney nodded and slipped out of the store. As soon as it shut behind her, Mr. Zoowalsky stirred and sat up. "Is she gone?"

Ty nodded. "Are you in pain? Did you hit your head?"

The clerk shook his head. "When she walked in, I thought I was a goner."

Yeah, I can relate to that, Ty thought. Something happened to him whenever he was around Laney, and he wasn't talking about fishing snakes out of drains or getting the contents of a watering can dumped over him.

She made something want to come to life within him. Something he had thought was pretty much dead. Her presence recharged and restored an essential part of him that had been absent for years, maybe a lifetime. She made him laugh and frustrated and baffled him. Above all, she made him aware that he cared for her.

At the same time, he was too much of a realist to believe that lasting happiness waited around the corner for him and Laney. She was engaged. Besides, he had vowed never to let himself become vulnerable to another woman, and he wasn't about to change his mind now.

She had to learn for herself that knowing how to make Rock's coffee or iron his shirts would not guarantee her a happy marriage, either, or even provide an unbreakable foundation for a great relationship. In truth, he didn't know how people stayed together.

The deepest kind of loneliness, he thought, was being in a relationship with the wrong person. He remembered all too well how he would pick up Anna Mae for a date in his car. She would sit beside him but look out the window. No matter how hard he tried, it always seemed as if her thoughts were a million miles away. Of course he couldn't tell Laney any of these things. He had no business interfering with her life.

It was the last thing he needed.

fifteen

Later that night, G. C. Varner called an emergency meeting at his house.

"Drink your tea," he ordered Laney. "You look green."

"I am green," Laney said. "My facial mask got left on too long." She stirred her tea slowly. "I'm so sorry, Dad, about what happened."

Thomas, Laney's youngest brother, passed the sugar bowl toward her. "The clerk is going to be fine. The heart monitor he's on is just a precaution."

Beside her, as close as the table leg would allow, Rock nudged her in a reassuring manner and caused her to jiggle the teacup and spill some of its contents. As she mopped the stain, her father cleared his throat.

"I don't have to tell you we have a situation on our hands."

Laney looked down. "I just wanted to use the pay phone."

"Even if tonight had never happened, we would still be having this meeting," he said. "Attempted robbery is nothing compared to conspiracy to murder."

Laney shot Rock a sideways glance. "What are you talking about?"

"We understand you're under a lot of pressure," her

father said slowly, "but you can't go around threatening people."

"Threatening people?" Laney's head shot up. "I haven't threatened anyone."

Her father gestured to Rock, who was smiling as if the expression were held in place by clothespins. "Tell her," he said.

"Mother has it in her head that you don't like her." Rock's smile dimmed a bit. "She thinks you might want to off her."

"Off her?" Laney blinked.

"You know." Rock shifted uncomfortably and drew his finger in a line across his throat.

"I can't believe she would think that about me," Laney cried, unexpectedly hurt.

"You can't argue with the facts, honey," Rock argued smoothly. "First there was the gerbil food incident."

Laney crossed her arms. "I didn't ask her to eat it, if that's what you're implying."

"You didn't stop her, either," Rock reminded her.

"It would be easier to flag down a 747 than stop your mother."

Thomas laughed, but Rock's expression remained neutral. "What about the way you tore up that bridesmaid's dress?"

"I wasn't threatening her," Laney protested.

"She wants a restraining order," Rock said. "Of course that was over the top, and I talked her out of it. I did, however, promise you'd get help."

"Help?" Laney repeated. The room had become warm despite the air-conditioning. She fanned herself. "She's the one who needs help if she thinks I was trying to off her." She stared at Rock in disbelief. "Don't you see what she's doing?"

Rock sighed wearily. "What is she doing?"

"She's trying to make you think I'm crazy so you won't marry me. She's never thought I was good enough for you."

The color in Rock's face deepened. "Maybe we should discuss this privately."

"You brought it up," Laney replied stubbornly.

Rock fiddled with his moustache, and then his fingers progressed to check the alignment of the hairs in his light brown eyebrows. "All right then. I think you were out of line with my mother."

Laney drew in her breath. "You're siding with your mother?"

"Not exactly. I don't think you're dangerous, just temporarily agitated." He smiled the donut smile Laney knew preceded a compliment. "You're high-strung. All women of good breeding are. You'll calm down after the first child."

Calm down? Well-bred? Laney glared at him. She wasn't a horse and, if she were temporarily agitated, he was the one causing it.

"Now, kids," her father broke in. "We've got damage control to do here."

Thomas leaned forward. "Laney, we know all this is premarital jitters."

"But," Rock broke in smoothly, "a man is in the hospital, and Mother is worried. She's even written her attorney a letter to be opened in the event of her death." He shrugged. "Laney had better hope Mother doesn't slip in the bathtub."

"I'm only five points behind Steele in the polls," Laney's father said. "Thomas's family values campaign is working. I can win if we can get past your premarital jitters."

Laney looked at the deep grooves that curved across his brow. She saw the yearning in his eyes to win the election and felt the old stirring in her to please him. At the same time, her pride was wounded by the way they treated her.

"I don't have premarital jitters," Laney stated. She drew her hand through her hair then turned to her father. "I can't believe you're taking his side."

He snorted and pushed his chair back an inch from the table. "I'm not taking anyone's side," he said. "I'm just trying to mediate a solution."

"You want to drug me."

"Mediate," Thomas said, "not *medicate.*"

"I know the difference," Laney snapped.

"Of course you do." Thomas laughed without humor. "We just want to make sure you're not going to come apart at Dad's municipal building dedication." He paused. "You won't, will you?"

"Of course I won't!" Laney cried.

Thomas looked at her steadily. "We all have a lot riding on this election," he said. "I don't have to tell you what will happen to my PR firm if Dad loses."

"So what do you want me to do?" Laney asked. She looked down at her folded hands, knowing her father didn't have the answer she sought. *So what do You want me to do?* she repeated silently. *I've messed up again, big time. Please tell me what it is You want. I thought I knew Your will for me, but I don't. I don't even know the man I'm going to marry as well as I thought.*

"First," her father said, "don't talk to any reporters about what happened at the Eat and Go. Second, you'll do whatever it takes to mend your relationship with Tilly. Last, you'll practice your introduction of me until you're blue in the face." He pointed to her green-tinted cheeks. "By blue, I mean that as an expression."

Laney flinched as her father's eyes bored into hers. "Do you have a problem with any of this, Laney?"

She longed to tell him to stop staring at her as if she had directly inspired every tornado that had ever touched down in Texas.

Laney looked down at the diamond shining on her finger. She'd thought that getting married would lead her to a better life, or at least to a much less lonely one. Instead, she felt more apart from everyone than ever.

She sighed and nodded. "I'll do my best."

The men at the table relaxed visibly. "Good," Rock said with relief in his voice, "because I've already set up a time with Mother for Saturday night. She's agreed to teach you how to make pancakes."

"I didn't think you liked pancakes," Laney said, frowning.

"I don't," Rock admitted. "It was the one thing I could

think of that didn't involve any sharp instruments."

"Oh, great," Laney muttered. "She's probably going to want me to wear a straitjacket instead of an apron."

It didn't help when Rock neither laughed nor disagreed with her.

sixteen

The next morning, Laney drove with Angel to Good Faith's undeveloped land and went in search of God's will by the pond where everything had started.

As the cool, dark water came into sight, some of the tightness seemed to leave Laney's chest. She filled her lungs with the pine-scented air. *Thank You, God, for the beauty of this place. Thank You for Mr. Zoowalsky's good doctor's report. I'm glad he's decided to attend church regularly from now on. Could You please help me find the person who wrote the note in church and help them?*

Suddenly Angel yelped joyfully and launched himself in the direction of a tall, broad-shouldered man who stood at the edge of the water.

Laney couldn't help feeling glad to see him. And Angel was surely happy about it.

"What are you doing here?" she asked.

"What are you doing here?" he asked in return. "I thought I told you not to come here by yourself. It's way too isolated."

Laney nodded. "That's exactly why I came." She sighed. "I needed a place to be alone. Everyone in town thinks what happened last night with that clerk is hilarious." She paused. "Well, almost everyone."

"I'm not laughing," Ty said gently. "Well, not anymore, that is."

"My dad is about to kill me," Laney added. "I don't even want to think about what he's going to say if the *Daily Destiny* writes the story." She shook her head. "And the worst thing is that I'm no closer to finding the person who wrote that note than when I started."

"Laney, all this will blow over. If your family doesn't realize what a great heart you have by now, they're crazy." He stepped closer to her. "Didn't Rock think you made a pretty cute Martian?"

"Actually, he thought I needed stress management sessions," Laney admitted. "Which is better than what my future mother-in-law thought. She told Rock I'm emotionally unstable." She tried to smile and make light of it. "And you know what that clerk at the convenience store called me—an angel of death."

"What happened last night wasn't a big deal," Ty said. "If you ask me, calling you an angel of death was a huge overstatement."

In the face of such sympathy, Laney felt her heart melt. "You're the first person who's said anything nice about what happened." She looked up at him. "Thank you, Ty."

He shrugged it off. "Maybe the next time you feel like going on a stakeout, you'd better call me."

"You'd go with me?"

"Of course."

"Seriously?"

"Seriously," Ty promised.

"Because you think I'd mess up without you."

He shook his head. "Because I want to help you. Because you're nice."

Laney felt her throat tighten. She fought to keep the tears down.

"You're a strong person, Laney. You'll see all this hoopla through."

Nobody but him had ever seen strength inside her. She smiled in gratitude. Something beautiful passed between them. She recognized it as friendship. Or was it? Was there something else in his eyes?

Laney took a step away from him. "Look—thanks for listening to me, but I'd better get going."

"Laney, wait."

She turned to go, but something in his voice stopped her. Then in the very deep distance she heard the roll of thunder.

She remembered her childhood illusions, how she had imagined she would hear the sound of thunder when she found the man of her dreams. She had long ago decided true love didn't happen that way.

Maybe Rock and her family were right—she had a huge case of premarital jitters, and this explained why her nerves felt jangled.

"The storm," Ty said. "It's coming fast."

The thunder rumbled again, louder now. The sky darkened, and she saw the first blink of lightning. The rain splattered them, sporadically at first. Big, fat drops fell heavily on their heads and shoulders. Ty looked over his shoulder and frowned. "We'd better run for it."

He dashed ahead of her into the shelter of the woods. Around them leaves pinged as raindrops exploded onto them. "Hurry," Ty urged her as they raced down the path she had just traveled.

The rain picked up, hurling pellets that filled the woods with a cacophony of sound, turned leaves a shade of deep, vibrant green, and lifted the sweet smell of rich earth.

Even as the rain soaked her, Laney felt like laughing. She drew in great breaths of the clean, sweet air, made cold by the storm. She delighted in the feel of the earth beneath her pounding feet and the challenge of racing the storm.

Ty reached his car first. Yanking the front door open, he waited for her to get inside then slammed it shut. Moments later he threw himself into the driver's seat.

Breathing hard, Laney sat listening to the rain pounding the roof of the car. She glanced at Ty but didn't speak. She didn't think she could be heard above the roar of the rain. Ty grinned, and she grinned back.

They were both out of breath, dripping wet, and completely at the mercy of the storm. And yet she felt exhilarated.

Lightning flashed in eye-dazzling forks of electricity so beautiful that Laney could only sit in wonder, completely in awe of the forces around them.

Part of her wished the storm would go on forever. She felt safe and comfortable. Even when the seconds between the lightning strikes lengthened into minutes, she sat still, listening to the drum of rain.

Finally Ty broke the silence between them. "That was some storm."

"It was beautiful, wasn't it?"

"You weren't scared?"

Laney shrugged. "I've always liked storms. Didn't anyone ever tell you thunder is just the angels bowling?"

"Not for a long time." Ty wiped his face with his shirtsleeve. "A storm can be dangerous. It's not something to romanticize about."

"I'm not," Laney said slowly, "but a storm can also have a purpose."

Ty snorted. "Tell that to someone who loses his home when a tornado hits it."

"I would tell that person God doesn't cause bad things to happen," Laney said. "And one thing I know is He can take any tragedy and turn it into triumph."

Ty looked at her. "Any tragedy?"

"Any tragedy," Laney confirmed. "You just need to have faith in Him."

Laney sensed something stirring within him and hoped it was an urge to embrace a belief that God was no farther away than the chambers of his heart.

Ty frowned as if he were considering her words hard. She could sense the silent struggle. She wanted to comfort him, to share her faith, and to help heal whatever scars still pained him.

"Don't you think it's time you told me about what's tearing you up inside?"

Ty looked away. He was quiet for so long that she thought he wouldn't answer her question. And then he began.

"We ran every morning at 5:30," he finally said, "at the high school's cross-country course. I pushed the pace even faster that morning, so when we got back to the school, both of us were doubled over in pain, which meant we'd had a great run."

As Ty continued his story, Laney closed her eyes and pictured the whole scene unfolding.

❧

Mickey reached over to tousle his younger brother's hair. "You should have been a distance runner, not a policeman."

Gasping for breath, Ty sank onto a concrete bench in a courtyard outside the cafeteria. "You're getting soft is all," he said. "Sitting around in a cushy teaching job."

He was only teasing. Both knew it.

"A cushy job is driving around all day in a squad car and eating donuts," Mickey replied when he had enough air. "The real work is teaching."

Ty made a snort of disagreement, although in his heart he agreed. Mickey taught with a passion and knowledge that had earned him a National Teacher's Award. At times he seemed so in touch with his students that he could have been reading their minds.

Ty walked over to an abstract concrete statue, which resembled a very confused cactus plant. He ran his hands over the grooves in the statue wondering what the drilled holes symbolized. He was about to make a flip remark when his hands touched something smooth and cylindrical.

"Check this out," Ty said, withdrawing his hand. "It's a bullet case."

There had been six bullet cases.

"We should report these," Ty said.

Mickey shook his head. He held the bullet casings in his hand and rolled them around. "It's probably just a joke."

Ty shook his head. "We shouldn't fool around with this."

"We won't," Mickey promised. "Just give me a day to put my feelers out. We'll find out more that way than if you drive up to the school in a tank and start leveling lockers."

The sweat dripped into Ty's eye. He wiped it with the back of his hand. All his instincts demanded immediate action. He looked at his older brother, trying not to be swayed by a lifetime of following Mickey's advice.

"I don't know," Ty said. "I don't like this."

Mickey smiled and flicked sweat off his arm at his brother. "Trust me," he said. "I know the kids here. They're good kids. All they need is a chance to prove that."

❧

"Two days later, two students walked into Fairmont High School, and six people died. Mickey died shielding one of the targeted boys with his body."

Sweat stung Ty's eyes, the way it had all those years ago when he had found the casings. His hand rubbed his aching eyes, smearing moisture onto already wet skin.

"Mickey would be alive if I'd insisted we go to the police right away. It's all my fault."

This was his secret, his guilt, the private pain he had not

allowed himself to share with anyone until now. He could barely bring himself to look at Laney.

"I'm so sorry about your brother," she said. Her eyes were full of a compassion he had never seen before. "But it wasn't your fault." She looked hard into his eyes and drew a shaky breath. "We may not understand why tragedies occur, but nothing happens by chance. We're all here for a reason."

Ty let out his breath in a huff. "I don't know what I believe anymore." He looked at her, his eyes still full of pain. "I heard a hawk cry out earlier today, just before you showed up at the lake."

"I saw it in the sky," she said.

"I followed one just like it at the high school," Ty continued. A distant part of himself begged him to shut up. "I ended up in an outdoor courtyard. I looked down and saw a drawing in the gravel." He paused. "Someone had sketched what looked like a bullet with a bunch of numbers inside." He looked down. "I wanted to search lockers for firearms."

"Why didn't you?"

"A drawing in the gravel isn't enough evidence."

She smiled at him. "What would be the harm in checking the lockers?"

"It would require a search warrant," Ty explained. "Even if I went over your father's head, no judge would grant one based on a crude drawing in the gravel."

"Did you copy down what you saw?"

Ty nodded. "It's in my wallet. There isn't much to see, just a bunch of numbers."

"Could the numbers be a student identification number?"

"No," Ty replied. "I checked. Student ID numbers have seven digits. This has more."

"How about a combination to a lock?"

Ty nodded. "Could be," he said. "I thought so, too. No way to be sure unless we access the records."

"Can't you just hack your way into the computer?"

Ty laughed. "Sure. That's about as likely as a firearms-sniffing dog showing up on my front step."

"What if you could do a locker-to-locker?" Laney insisted. "What if you had a firearms-sniffing dog at your disposal? Would you do it?"

An unlawful search? Ty couldn't believe his ears. Did she think he was crazy? "Of course I wouldn't," he said. "You think I want to do something illegal just weeks before the election?"

"You don't have to ask my father for a bomb-sniffing dog. We have one right here in Destiny."

Ty frowned. "We do?"

"Yes, it's Angel."

Ty laughed. "Angel?"

Laney's chin lifted. "Angel is a graduate of the Canine Development Center in Austin. It was a perk of Dad's job. Anyway, Angel passed the bomb-sniffing course with flying colors."

"You trained a papillon to be a police dog?"

Laney nodded. "We've never had to use him before. But it's only been about five years. I'm sure Angel hasn't forgotten a thing."

Ty rubbed his hands over his face hard. "That little weenie dog can sniff out gunpowder?"

"With 99.9 percent accuracy," Laney said. "The instructor in Austin was very impressed."

"I can't believe I'm hearing this," Ty said.

"So when do we do the locker-to-locker search?"

Was he actually considering this? He bit down on his lower lip hard and ordered himself to get a grip.

After a moment, Ty sighed. "Saturday."

"Will you have a key, or are we going in through a window?"

"Neither," Ty said grimly. "We'll pick the lock."

seventeen

Three days later, Ty drove his car into the high school parking lot. He spotted Laney instantly, standing beside her van and looking barely old enough to drive it. In her arms, Angel appeared to be the size of a football, and Ty imagined the dog couldn't have a brain much larger than a pea. He fought the urge to drive right past Laney, past the expectant smile on her face, and past the button-bright eyes of the papillon. He wanted to gun the motor and head back into the land of sanity where there was no risk of hurting his professional reputation.

He rubbed his chin impatiently. It didn't help that he had never seen a woman who looked less likely to find a gun in a locker than Laney did. She looked fragile and innocent, vulnerable and slightly lost in the nearly empty parking lot.

He jerked the car into gear and swung into the parking spot next to Laney's minivan. Because his heart jumped when she smiled at him, he scowled as fiercely as he could.

"Angel is ready," Laney said. She must have given the dog an unseen signal, because it began waving its paw at him gaily. Ty frowned at the papillon. Drug-, bomb-, and firearms-sniffing canines did not wave at people.

"He's very pleased to help," Laney continued. The little dog yipped as if in affirmation.

Ty's frown increased with the ridiculous thought that the dog would see his expression and imitate it. The hairy football, however, grinned at him. Ty shook his head. It was those ears, huge, upright wings, that gave the dog no credibility whatsoever. This wasn't the sort of dog that could save a school from a shooting. It looked like a small cat could beat the stuffing out of it.

"Maybe this isn't such a good idea," Ty said tactfully. "Five years is a long time for a dog to remember everything about sniffing out weapons."

"Don't worry," Laney said. "If a gun is in the building, Angel will find it. I hid my father's M-54 under my mattress for practice. Angel found it in five minutes."

"That's not a gun," Ty said. He was so surprised his face twisted in horror. "That's a bazooka. Do you realize if that gun went off, it could shoot through two floors?"

"It's not a bazooka," Laney corrected calmly. "It's classified as an automatic handgun."

Ty grunted to indicate he disregarded her definition. Didn't she realize she could have blown off her head? "What was your father thinking to let you borrow it?"

Laney looked briefly at the ground then back up at Ty, who groaned. "Tell me you didn't steal the gun from him."

"I didn't steal the gun," Laney said softly. "I borrowed it." She paused. "I'll put it back tonight."

Ty slapped his forehead with his hand. "This is just great," he said. "Why search the school for illegal firearms when we can find a stolen M-54 under your mattress?"

"It's not under my mattress anymore," Laney informed him, looking smug. "It's in the front seat of the minivan, inside the lasagna pan I borrowed from Mother Tilly."

"That's supposed to make me feel better?" Ty frowned down at her. "I can just see you hitting a pothole and taking down a helicopter."

Laney raised her hand to shield her eyes from the sun. "Very funny. I happen to hold the 1985 Junior Miss Sharpshooter title for the state of Texas."

Ty drew an exaggerated breath, as if this news were monumental. "No wonder Mother Tilly is scared," he said.

Laney frowned. "She doesn't have to worry, and neither do you. I know all about safety catches."

"When I'm around you, there is no such thing as safety," Ty muttered. "I'm beginning to feel sorry for Rock."

"Fine," Laney said. "Feel sorry for him all you want, but spare me the details." She turned on her heel and shot him a look. "I've got lockers to search."

Ty waited until her back was fully turned before he released the smile he'd been struggling to hide for the last five minutes. He wanted to shake her for playing with guns; at the same time, he wanted to laugh until his ribs ached. He could accuse her of many things, but he couldn't deny that when he was around her the blood pumped gladly through his veins, the air sang in his lungs, and the sunlight held an electric touch on his skin.

For a moment, he allowed himself to imagine that light coming into his house, blasting away the shadows, filling the empty spaces with something that had been absent for a long time—the sense of joy.

And then he reminded himself that she was engaged to another man and her father was his opponent in a close race for sheriff. And if that wasn't enough, he'd been left at the altar and cleaned out financially.

Holding these thoughts firmly, Ty pushed the smile to the back of his mind, arranged his features into his best professional scowl, and walked toward the front door of the high school.

Ty studied the locked doorway for a moment then took a slim tool out of his pocket. He inserted the piece of metal into the keyhole, twisting and simultaneously throwing his shoulder against the door. With a loud popping sound, the door flung open.

When they entered the building, Ty's heart began to pound. Everything his eyes took in—the glossy, waxed floors; the walls painted an ugly, toxic green; the stainless steel water fountain—reminded him of another school and another time.

For once, he welcomed the ghosts that swirled around him. A sour smell filled Ty's nostrils. "What's that smell?" Ty looked at Angel suspiciously.

"It's not Angel," Laney replied. "Maybe it's the school." She lifted the hair off the back of her neck with her one free hand. "It's hot in here. They must have turned the air-conditioning down for the weekend." She held the dog in the air, just under Ty's nose. "Here, take a whiff."

The last thing Ty wanted to do was smell the hairy dog

raised like a sacrifice to his nose. He had no choice, however, but to sniff the dog that was close enough to lick his face and who proceeded to do exactly that. Although he made a sound of disgust, the hot pink tongue that washed his face comforted him. "Some police dog," he muttered. "Probably aced the classes in licking criminals to death."

Laney giggled softly. "Nope, but he was the only dog in his class that could do a handstand."

Ty stopped in his tracks. "What?"

Laney tugged his arm. "Come on. Do you want to check lockers or not?"

"Yes, but with a dog that does handstands?"

"He has many talents." She took a step forward. "Let's get going. We've got a lot of ground to cover."

Ty shrugged off the feeling of impending doom and followed her. He was only too glad to get off the subject of the dog. "You seem to know your way around here pretty well."

"I went to school here," Laney replied. "And you know our church meets in the gymnasium." She pointed to a door on their right. "There's the biology classroom. Want to see the exact spot where I threw up when we were dissecting frogs?"

"I'll pass on that," Ty said, swallowing hard his own memory of hundreds of frogs hopping out of the biology classroom as Mickey triumphantly herded them to safety.

Coming to the double doors, Ty stopped Laney again and peered covertly into the dark recesses of the stairwell. Satisfied that all was clear, he moved them up the stairs to the second floor.

Starting at the far left of the building, they began searching lockers.

It was slow work. First Laney let Angel sniff the bottom of the locker, and then she held him up to the vents so he could smell the upper half. The little dog moved slowly around the perimeters of the lockers, his big ears upright and alert, his black nose delicately brushing the metal surfaces.

For the most part, Ty watched with his arms crossed. He had a feeling they were on a wild goose chase, that even if the contents necessary to build an atom bomb were within one of these lockers, Angel would walk right past it. That meant he was there for only one reason, and that reason was standing right in front of him. The thought did little to improve his mood.

He disciplined himself not to speak to her for the first thirty minutes, and then he got bored with the silence. "So how's the studying for the premarital exam going?"

Laney lifted the dog. "Fine," she said. "We've been through three volumes of the cookbooks."

Ty grinned. "What about studying things about you? Does he know about you being a black belt and winning that sharpshooting title and Angel's degree from doggie Quantico?"

Laney swallowed visibly. Ty tried not to enjoy her look of discomfort. She didn't have to tell him Rock didn't know these things; he saw it in her eyes. He was about to continue teasing her when he heard a noise.

"Get Angel," he hissed at Laney. "Someone's coming."

After giving Ty a quick, agonized look at the thought of discovery, Laney sprang into action. She ran after Angel, startling the dog so badly he bolted. "Angel!" she called.

Ty turned at the panic in her voice. He watched the dog disappear down the long corridor. He twisted the knob of a nearby classroom and found it locked. "Forget the dog," he ordered.

Other classrooms proved to be locked. Now the sound of footsteps echoed more loudly, and he heard the click of a door opening.

Ty tried another door. As it swung open, he pulled Laney inside a small, dark room. He banged his head on a shelf and knocked a roll of toilet paper into the metal bucket at his feet. Two brooms hit him in the back of the head as he wiggled deeper into the shallow closet, pulling Laney after him.

A metal bucket was between his feet, and an electric floor polisher pressed into his leg. The room smelled of disinfectants and detergent. Laney's head brushed his shoulder, smelling of lilacs and summer, sunshine, and something so faint he bent closer, trying to define it.

He ordered himself to pull back, as if he commanded troops that faced sure and complete annihilation if the retreat were not imminent.

"Ty?"

He heard Angel whine just outside the door. The dog must have heard Laney's voice.

"Ty?"

Pressing himself deeper into the closet, he bumped a

shelf. The next thing he knew, something hard clunked him on the top of his head.

"Ouch." He instantly promised never to purchase powdered cleanser again, if that's what the can turned out to be.

Laney giggled. "Are you okay?"

Before he could reply, the door to the broom closet swung open. A small woman with big hair teased into a great yellow bouffant stared back at him.

"Mrs. Henley!" Laney exclaimed in a voice so falsely bright that Ty cringed. "How nice to see you again." Laney stepped out of the broom closet with her chin held high. Ty caught the push broom before it hit her in the back.

The muscles in the older woman's neck quivered before any words came out. "Laney Varner? What are you doing in that broom closet? And who is this man?"

"Detective Ty Steele," Ty said, deftly stepping around the tipped metal bucket and ignoring the can of cleanser that rolled out behind him.

Mrs. Henley's eyes narrowed from behind her red, wire-rimmed glasses. "You're the one running for sheriff." Her right eyebrow arched. "I'm sure there's a good reason for all that clanging around in the broom closet."

Laney turned brick red. "It's not what you think," she said.

"We're here on police business," Ty said, aware of how absurd this sounded yet saying it anyway.

"Police business?" Mrs. Henley asked. "I suppose you're checking to see if our electric floor buffer is up to code."

Laney threw her shoulders back. "Detective Steele and

I are spot-checking lockers," she said. "Our canine officer is on site."

"Canine officer?"

Laney pointed at the papillon that had recovered from its fright and now nosed curiously around the principal's ankles.

The older woman squinted at the dog. "That's a canine officer?" She sniffed. "And underneath this gray suit I'm wearing a Wonder Woman costume."

The thought of the strict principal in a superhero costume nearly undid Ty. Before he could stop himself, he glanced sideways at Laney, who had her hand smashed over her mouth. As their gazes met, Laney's face attained the deepest shade of red he'd ever seen.

"You may joke, ma'am," Ty said quietly, "but we've received an anonymous tip that one of your students may be hiding arms on the premises."

Mrs. Henley put her hands on her hips. "A student hiding guns? No way. Somebody is playing a joke here." She looked pointedly at Ty.

"It's no joke," Ty replied.

"I suppose your tip told you there were machine guns in the broom closet?" The woman's hairdo seemed to puff out in a mute statement of incredulity.

Laney looked at the ground. Her shoulders shook. This didn't help Ty's own suicidal urge to laugh. Since when had he lost his senses? "I can assure you we're here on police business."

Mrs. Henley's eyes blinked rhythmically as she considered

Ty's words. She frowned as Ty held her gaze without flinching. Angel, evidently bored from the discussion, trotted down the aisle. He began sniffing at the lockers then stopped in front of one and began to bark.

"That's his cry!" Laney said in amazement. "He's found something."

"It's illegal to search a locker without a warrant," the principal said. Her eyes hardened. "Come back with a search warrant."

"Are you sure?" Ty said. "The dog smells something."

"I can smell a rat, too," Mrs. Henley said.

"It wouldn't hurt to look," Laney urged quietly. "If something did happen, how could you live with yourself?"

Ty leaned closer to the principal. "It could be a Glock or a pair of ripe gym socks in there." He pulled a piece of worn paper from his wallet and unfolded it carefully. "I copied this from a drawing I found in the school courtyard." He paused while she examined the drawing. "You still want to bet there's a pair of moldy socks in there?"

She studied Ty's eyes for a long time, and then she nodded her agreement. "We'll look, but if this is a practical joke, you'll both get detention until Christmas!"

eighteen

Ty stepped around the excited dog to examine locker B-2003. It looked exactly like the other battered gray lockers surrounding it, give or take a dent. "Step back," Ty ordered as Laney and Mrs. Henley peered over his shoulder.

Frowning in concentration, Ty entered the numbers from the drawing he'd found in the gravel. After he'd entered the last number, he pulled the handle. The lock held. Frowning, Ty tried variations of the number but met with the same result.

Mrs. Henley's right eyebrow arched. "I'm sure this is pointless." She paused. "But since you'll probably open it with a crowbar if I don't get the combination, I'll help you."

As the principal shuffled off, Ty turned to Laney. "Are you sure Angel knows what he's doing?"

Laney looked at Angel, who sat at attention in front of the locker. "Yes."

"Because we could call it all off right now."

"I'm sure," Laney said.

"Okay then."

Laney leaned against a locker. The metal felt cool and hard on her back. She thought about how they had hid in the broom closet. When the can of cleanser had rolled out behind Ty, her ribs had ached with the need to laugh. She wondered if it was too late for her and Rock to have fun together or if their lives would always be as respectable and predictable as she had thought she wanted.

Could she go through with her marriage to Rock? She liked him and admired his relationship with God. But she wondered if this was what God wanted for her.

She shot a glance at Ty. He looked like such a tough guy leaning up against the lockers, an aging football player who could still muscle his way through life.

When she had discovered the note in church, she had been so sure she had been given a chance to help someone who needed it. Now, however, she had begun to realize that she herself might be the one who needed help.

A low growl erupted from Angel, announcing the principal's return. Bending, Laney smoothed the ridge of hair that had arisen along the dog's back. She frowned thoughtfully. Usually Angel only reacted like this when—

Her jaw dropped open. Not only had Mrs. Henley returned, but she had also brought along Rock and her father.

Even at this distance, she could see the disapproval in the tight set of her father's mouth. As they halted in front of the locker, he addressed Ty. "You think there's a gun in the locker?" He drawled the words sarcastically, as if this were as likely as finding Barney the dinosaur.

Ty colored but held the older man's gaze. "Won't know what's inside until we open it."

"I want to talk to you alone." Her father's voice came from nearly immobile lips, another sure sign of his anger. Laney's stomach clenched as the two of them set off together.

"What you all were doing wasn't right," the principal stated, "so I called the sheriff."

"Laney." Rock gently touched her arm. "What are you doing here?"

His eyebrows lifted in what might have been an expression of concern and support.

Laney tried to arrange her features into the composed expression of a person completely in charge of her senses, as if conducting an illegal locker search with a seven-pound papillon in an empty high school was an ordinary occurrence. "Looking for guns."

"Steele put you up to this, didn't he?" Rock didn't wait for her answer. "Don't you see this has everything to do with the election? Your father's reelection is important to me, Laney," he whispered. "It's important to us."

"So is stopping a school shooting," Laney said. She ran her fingers through her hair, knowing it was hopeless to make him understand.

"Laney, you belong in your pet shop, not on a SWAT team." The tips of his moustache quivered. "You're aligning yourself with your father's chief rival."

"I'm not aligning myself with anyone," Laney said, holding his gaze. "I'm trying to do the right thing."

Rock drew back. "This isn't my Laney talking to me," he said. He searched her face with a mixture of disappointment and suspicion.

"I never told you, Rock, but Angel went to the Canine Development Center in Austin. He's trained to sniff out firearms."

A ripple of emotion passed over his face as Rock made his disbelief obvious. "Sure," he said. "He probably was Rin Tin Tin's body double, too." He laughed loudly.

"That's why I didn't tell you before," Laney said. Her

fists clenched. "I knew you'd make a big joke about it. You always do."

"Well, honey," Rock said, "that's what I love about you. The way you make me laugh." His expression softened as he looked into her eyes. "Let's not fight about this. You're not yourself, and it's because you're stressed out about the premarital exam." He stroked her cheek. "You're going to ace it this time. Even my mother couldn't tell your lasagna from hers in the taste test last night."

Laney's chin lifted. "This isn't about the exam or the lasagna. Angel may have found a gun."

Rock's eyebrows quivered. Laney fought the urge to reach up and physically hold them in place.

"There are no guns in that locker," Rock said firmly. "If you believe there are, you need more help than I thought." He reached for Laney's arm. "Let's go."

"Angel smells firearms in that locker," Laney insisted.

"That dog couldn't scent a firecracker if it went off under his nose," Rock said.

"There are guns," Laney said. "I just know it."

At her words, Rock released Laney's arm and fingered his moustache thoughtfully. His eyebrows calmed, and a spark of interest appeared in his eyes. "If I look in that locker and don't find a gun in there, will you agree to take some stress management courses?"

Laney's chin lifted at the challenge. "I will."

"Okay," Rock said. Turning, he called down the hallway. "Come on, G. C. Stop giving Steele a hard time and open up this locker."

nineteen

"It's at your discretion, Beulah," Laney's father said. An angry-looking flush had spread across his weathered brown cheeks. "We've got no warrant or just cause to open it."

"We'll open the locker," the principal said. She smiled at Laney. "My cousin is a family counselor. If you turn out to need it, I can give you his number."

Ty turned to Laney. "What's that all about?"

Laney tried not to squirm under Ty's intense stare. She couldn't simply blurt out that if Angel didn't find weapons in the locker, she'd promised to take stress management classes.

As Ty's glance lingered on Laney, Rock's arm slipped proprietarily around Laney's waist. "It's private."

The muscles in Ty's jaw tightened.

Before Laney could explain, Beulah swung the locker door open.

A poster of Jimi Hendricks stared at them from the back of the door. A long tear ran from the bottom of the poster past Hendricks's knees.

Her gaze drifted to the blue and red nylon running jacket that hung on a hook beside a dark blue T-shirt. A stack of books sat on the shelf, and a brown paper bag lay wedged between a pair of high-top, black sneakers and a half-filled water bottle.

Angel yipped in triumph as Ty examined the stack of

books, ranging from a textbook promising all the joys biology had to offer to an existential novel by Kafka.

Ty reached for the paper bag at the bottom of the locker. He lifted it gently out of the locker as Angel barked wildly.

"That's Angel's noise when he's made a find!" Laney cried.

"Okay, everyone," Ty said. "Stand back."

Laney hung on to Angel's collar as the small dog strained to stick his nose in the evidence bag.

First, Ty pulled out a can of soda. Next he pulled out a rectangular shape wrapped in aluminum foil. He carefully peeled back one side. "Meatball wedge."

Rewrapping the wedge, he then pulled out a large bag of corn chips, two chocolate cupcakes, and a banana more black than yellow.

Ty replaced the lunch and meticulously inspected the windbreaker's pockets. When this yielded nothing more than spare change and gum wrappers, he turned to the stack of books and flipped through each.

Beside her, Rock nudged Laney. "Congratulations. Your bloodhound has saved the school from a meatball wedge."

Laney's stomach flip-flopped. "Check the lunch again," she said. "There has to be some kind of mistake."

"Right," Rock said. "We'd better make sure those are real meatballs."

"There is no mistake," her father said. He put his hands on his hips and faced Laney. "The dog found food, not arms."

Laney released Angel from his leash. "Go on, boy," she urged. "Find." The dog lunged forward and pounced on the bag with the determination of a terrier digging out from under a fence.

Her father swooped the little dog in his arms and then handed him to Rock. "There's your proof, Laney," he said gruffly. "The dog wants to eat the evidence." He smiled apologetically at Mrs. Henley. "Do you want to press charges for breaking and entering?" His gray eyebrows arched. "I wouldn't blame you if you did."

The principal appeared to give it a thought then shook her head. "No."

The older man nodded. "In that case, Detective Steele, you're on desk duty until further notice, pending a full investigation."

"But, Dad," Laney protested, "it wasn't his fault. I talked him into letting Angel search the school." She squeezed her father's forearm. "I still think we should search some more."

Rock and her father exchanged looks of agreement, and Laney knew her fate was sealed. "The only thing you'll be searching for is a complete explanation of what happened here today." Her father pointed his index finger at her. "Which you will begin in my car."

"Dad," Laney said, "we have to keep searching." She looked at Ty for support. "Tell him about the drawing."

Her father stared hard at her. "In my car. Now."

When he got like this, her father didn't hear or see her. He looked through her, and her voice passed through him unheard. Laney felt a familiar frustration rise.

"I'm serious," Laney insisted. "Don't let the way you feel about me get in the way of doing what's right."

Her father rolled his eyes. "For the last time, there is no

reason to believe there are guns in the school." He didn't bother to conceal the exasperation in his eyes. "You are coming with me."

Laney gave Ty a look of appeal. "Are you just going to stand there?"

"Your father's right," Ty said. "Our search is over."

Their friendship was over, too. She saw it in the way he looked right through her, the same way he had the very first time she had met him. A sense of loss slammed through her. Her heart ached with the realization she had done what he had feared most. She'd inadvertently created a scandal that might cost him the election.

Who was going to vote for a man who conducted illegal locker searches that netted nothing more than a meatball sandwich?

Lord? I've done it again, messed things up completely. Ty Steele needs You, Laney prayed. Please help him. You can do miracles, and it's going to take one to make this right.

❧

Ty Steele jabbed the button that controlled the air-conditioning in his squad car. Cold air immediately blasted from the car's vents but did nothing to stem the sweat that poured down his back.

He blamed the air-conditioner and then the hot weather for his discomfort. Most of all, he blamed himself for trusting a civilian and a rat-sized dog to do police work.

Over and over he imagined the laughter that had followed when Angel discovered nothing more than a meatball sandwich.

This, he reminded himself, was what happened when he stopping thinking like a policeman. Instead of looking for firearms, he'd been looking at Laney's face. He, who had always prided himself on his professionalism, had acted in the most unprofessional way and at the worst possible time.

He'd stepped forward in faith, wanting to believe for the first time since his brother's death that there was a reason for it. That God had allowed Mickey's death in order to prevent other deaths and that He would use Ty as an instrument. The anger and guilt he'd carried around for so long had finally disappeared. In its place, Ty had found the reawakening of his faith, and it had felt comforting and familiar. For once, it seemed, he would trust God to lead him where he needed to be.

His step of faith, however, had placed his career in jeopardy. He didn't know how to begin to fix the damage. Going backward wasn't an option. Nothing he could do would change what had happened. What then?

More sweat rolled down the back of his shirt. He wiped his hands on his pants and tried to lighten his grip on the wheel.

He didn't want to surrender control of his life. Didn't want to make himself vulnerable by depending on anything or anyone else. He'd spent the past few years perfecting this ability.

His power to separate himself from his emotions had driven Anna Mae crazy. She'd wanted picnics, long walks, and even longer conversations. When Mickey died, Anna Mae had been relentless, coming at him from every angle to talk to her. Strangely, the more she accused him of having no emotions, the deeper she drove him into himself.

He realized now that he hadn't loved Anna Mae as

much as she needed to be loved. Strangely, the knowledge of his own culpability freed him of the lingering traces of hurt that had consumed him.

You've stepped forward in faith. Now what are you going to do? Go back to your empty house? Salvage your career by letting Laney take the blame for the illegal search?

The detective slammed the brakes just in time to avoid rear-ending the car in front of him. His tires shrieked on the hot pavement, but he ignored the looks of the drivers around him.

He'd rather quit the force than blame Laney. She deserved to be loved, honored, and cherished by a man worthy of her. If that rat, Rock Weyeth, didn't treat her right, he'd answer to Ty. Ty would make himself forget any other thoughts he'd had. They were just a momentary lapse, an aberration in a life punctuated with logical and cool, calm reasoning.

Something deep inside seemed to cry out with a need he'd denied for a long time. His fingers clenched the steering wheel as his heart pounded in his chest. He thought about how empty and hard the last few years had been. Pulling off to the side of the road, Ty sat for a long time, weighing his options. Finally he closed his eyes. *Okay, Lord. I've tried to do it my way for a long time. Now I'm giving myself to You. We'll do it Your way. What do I do next?*

twenty

"Do you feel like you're back in high school?" Pastor Bruce asked Laney as she and Rock walked into the classroom. They had arrived at the school in order to take another premarital exam. "One of these days our church will be built," the pastor continued, "but until then we're here."

Laney settled into the third row. Rock sat in the row in front of her.

"Here we go," Pastor Bruce said cheerfully as he passed out the exam. He glanced at the clock. "You have thirty minutes."

Gripping her pencil, Laney stared at the first multiple-choice question. "What color are your fiancé's eyes?" Sighing, Laney shifted in her seat. Did the pastor mean with or without his tinted contacts? Rock wore blue-tinted lenses, but without them his eyes were a muddy, indiscriminate color. The three choices were blue, gray, or brown. She frowned. The correct answer could be any of those. She guessed brown.

She studied the next question. "What color is your fiancé's hair?" Worrying her lower lip, Laney decided this had to be a trick question. Did the pastor mean before Rock highlighted it? Brow furrowed, Laney selected "dark brown."

"What is your fiancé's favorite food?" Rock's favorite food depended on the meal and time of the day. Laney remembered Mother Tilly had said beef bourguignon was his favorite. Yet the other night he'd praised her lasagna dish and claimed it was his new favorite. The third choice, a fruit smoothie, was hardest still. Rock's favorite breakfast was a fruit smoothie. She picked the lasagna because she thought that was what he would pick.

She plowed steadily through the exam. *God, please help me get through this exam,* she prayed. *Rock is a good servant of Yours, and we could do Your work together. But something inside me doesn't want to marry him. Is that something You?*

The words blurred on the exam. Even the questions about her appeared difficult to answer. Rubbing her eyes, Laney struggled to concentrate. Her world seemed to be spinning out of control. Ever since that awful scene at the high school, everything had gone steadily downhill.

Her brothers had stopped teasing her and now treated her with a deference she found infuriating. At least once a day her father stopped in the store to check on her. Ty had disappeared from her life as abruptly as he'd entered it. And Rock, well, he still seemed to like her, but deep inside she knew he hadn't forgiven her for the most recent unfortunate incident with Mother Tilly.

Consumed with Angel's inexplicable failure at the high school, Laney had neglected to tell Rock about the gun in the lasagna pan. Tilly had discovered the gun and become convinced Laney had threatened her yet again. She'd called Rock to come over and make sure the gun wasn't loaded.

Somehow, in the process of handling the gun, and here Rock hadn't been very clear, it had gone off. Although no one had been injured, the shot had shattered the crystal chandelier in the foyer.

Laney shuddered. Rock had asked her about a hundred times how she could have forgotten the gun. She had no answer. Rock's chuckle from the row in front of her drew her attention back to the exam.

One question remained, a true or false. She stared at the bold letters. "Do you love him?"

She closed her eyes, suddenly knowing her feelings for Rock were not deep enough to marry him. *This is urgent, Lord,* she prayed. *I don't want to hurt Rock, but I can't marry him.*

"Time's up," Pastor Bruce said. Standing, he collected their papers. "You can wait while I grade them."

Laney jumped when Rock's hand landed on her shoulder.

"Can you believe that test?" Rock whispered. "Only a complete idiot could have failed that." He grinned at Laney. "And to think of all the time we spent studying."

Laney pulled hard at the diamond. Her knuckle seemed to have grown a size, and the skin strained and reddened as she pulled. "Rock, we need to talk."

"I know it," he said. "Where are we going to celebrate passing the test?"

"Can we go somewhere private?"

He chuckled. "You know how I feel about waiting for the wedding."

Laney said, "Rock, there's something you should know."

Rock's smile dimmed. "Does this have something to do with my mother?" He slipped an arm around her shoulder. "When you give her grandchildren, Mother's going to forget all about the chandelier."

Waving her hand, Laney replied, "Of course this isn't about your mother."

"Good," Rock said in relief. "I can't handle anything else."

Pastor Bruce cleared his throat. "Folks, I've finished grading the exams." He looked from Rock's face to Laney's. "You failed again."

"Failed?" Rock's eyes bulged. "You can't be serious."

"I'm sorry," Pastor Bruce replied. Standing, he smiled apologetically at them. "I'll leave you alone to discuss the results."

"How could you fail that test?" Rock seemed stunned.

Laney looked at his indignant face. "I think we both failed."

Rock appeared not to hear her. He looked at the questions she'd missed. "Laney, how could you miss the questions about my favorite foods?"

Laney shook her head. "I'm sorry."

Rock frowned. "You did it on purpose, didn't you? You're trying to get me back because of the stress management thing." He eyed her with a knowing look. "You gave me your word, young lady."

Laney yanked harder at the ring. "This isn't about the stress management sessions. I'm trying to tell you I can't marry you."

"Of course you can," Rock said. "We'll just have to take

another test. Maybe we can have an oral exam since the written ones seem to stress you out."

Laney shook her head. "Our engagement is off, Rock." She struggled with the ring. "I'm sorry."

"It can't be off," Rock argued. "We have too much invested in this relationship."

Laney watched the disbelief play across Rock's classic features. His skin reddened, and his eyes narrowed. She looked at the tiled floor. "It's nothing you did or said. It's this feeling that we have different paths to take in our lives."

Gesturing with his arm, Rock drew a large circle in the air. "We're so close to a great life together. All we have to do is reach out and grab it." His gaze locked with hers.

"I'm sorry," Laney said. "I'm really, really sorry." The ring dug into her skin as she yanked it off. The pain on her finger was nothing compared to the tightness of her heart. She wished she loved Rock enough to marry him, but she didn't.

For a moment, Rock stared at the ring, and then he looked at Laney. His eyes darkened, and his cheeks flushed a deep red. "I thought that even with all your faults, Laney, you could keep a promise." Rock lifted his chin. "I was wrong about you."

Slamming the classroom door, Rock stormed into the hallway. Laney listened to his footsteps, angry and loud then becoming more distant, until the noise faded away completely.

❧

Night had fallen when Laney left the high school. Throwing

her shoulders back, she pushed forward. Her leather shoes made a hollow clicking sound on the sidewalk.

Within the spill of light from an overhead street lamp, Laney marveled at the thickness of the night, the way an oak leaf curled at the tips, the beauty of the ordinary painted in dark gray shades of evening.

She'd done the right thing. Rock had been her safety net for a long time, and she would miss the security of the relationship he offered. But she didn't want to be treated like a child any longer and didn't want everyone to rescue her at every opportunity. She was perfectly capable of looking after herself.

Suddenly Laney felt acutely aware of God's presence. She might be alone, yet somehow He was with her, guiding her, giving her hope and confidence. She closed her eyes and inhaled deeply, filling her lungs and drawing the promise of her faith into her heart.

She felt Him directing her toward something more important than anything she had ever faced in her life. Every step brought her closer to a fulfillment of a plan that had been created long before she was ever born. *Please, God*, she prayed, *show me Your plan. I'll do my best not to mess it up.*

twenty-one

"You've been practicing the speech I wrote, right?" Thomas tried to sound calm, but his smile jerked sporadically.

Laney ignored the question. "Don't worry, Tommy." She straightened his best tie—a red designer tie she knew he wore only for the most important of client meetings—and patted his blue wool suit. "I'm not going to fall apart on you."

"Good," Thomas said. "You've got the paper I wrote?"

Laney nodded. "In my pocket."

She smoothed the thin fabric of her brown silk pants and felt the rustle of paper within her pocket. Along with the speech, she carried around the crumpled yellow paper she had found at the church. Although she hadn't made any progress in finding the writer, she hadn't forgotten her promise.

Absently she touched the little silver cross at her throat as her gaze traveled around the foyer of the new municipal building. People filled the lobby and spilled over into the corridors. Standing about in small groups, they chatted and laughed, their voices blurring into an indistinguishable rumble. Police officers milled about, along with judges and secretaries and administrators, all standing shoulder to shoulder.

"Any questions?" Thomas asked. "You know how to work the microphone?"

"Yes," Laney said.

"So you're ready."

"I'm ready to throw up," Laney replied. When she saw panic in her brother's face, she added, "Only kidding. Don't worry."

His muscles relaxed, and he looked hard into her eyes. "When I get nervous about public speaking, I look for one friendly face in that crowd, and then I'm okay." His eyes crinkled with warmth. "You can look for me, Laney."

Laney squeezed his hands. "Thanks, Tommy. You're the best."

"I know this is going to be tough for you, especially after breaking your engagement."

Laney nodded, grateful that her brother, more than anyone else in the family, had accepted her decision not to marry Rock. Thomas had not asked for details of the breakup with Rock, yet he had defended her loyally.

Thomas smiled at his sister, the lines of his mouth momentarily softening. "In my opinion, you should have dumped Rock a long time ago."

"Speaking of Rock," Laney said, "here he comes."

As Rock walked into sight, Thomas automatically stepped closer to his sister. Rock moved past them without speaking. His entire attention was centered on a tall, painfully thin man with a long neck that jutted forward like the neck of a turtle coming out of its shell.

"That's Judge Gray," Thomas muttered. "He's probably

filling his ear with how you tried to off his mother with the M-54 in the lasagna pan."

Laney shrugged. "It doesn't matter." Strangely it didn't. She, who had once cared so greatly about people's respect and opinion, had discovered it wasn't so important after all. Rock could tell everyone she had rabies and howled at the moon. As long as people were talking about her, they would leave Ty alone. She gladly would take full responsibility for the fruitless locker search if it meant removing the blemish from Ty's record.

Suddenly someone's warm hand touched Laney's arm. She turned and saw Ty Steele standing there. "Ty?"

The small lines around his mouth etched deeper into his face. His eyes, dark and deep-set, had tiny red lines of fatigue. "We need to talk," he said.

Laney nodded, but Thomas frowned. "You don't have time to go anywhere," he said. "We're just waiting for Dad to give the word before we start."

Ty pulled a worn paper from his pocket. "This can't wait." He spoke as if he and Laney were alone. "As I was driving here, I remembered what you had said about miracles, about asking for one." His eyes held hers in a steady gaze. "So I did."

Laney nodded. "You asked."

"And nothing happened," Ty said. "Instead, I kept having a nagging feeling I'd missed something about the locker search." He lowered his voice. "We didn't search the corn chip bag. There could have been bullets inside. It was heavy enough. And there's something else, too."

Thomas laughed. "Bullets in the corn chip bag?" He shook his head. "You'll have to come up with something better than that. Even Laney would never believe something so farfetched."

Even Laney? She wanted to step hard on her brother's shoe.

Ty scowled. "I figured out the code. It's so obvious."

Her father walked over to join them. He frowned on seeing Ty Steele—maybe because she was standing so close to him. "You ready, honey?" He took Laney's arm and pulled gently. "I'll walk you to the podium."

"The numbers on the paper were a time," Ty said, ignoring her father. "If I'm right, something could happen about fifteen minutes from now. We can't waste a second."

"Do you see how he's trying to use you, Laney?" Thomas's eyebrows nearly touched his hairline. "If you leave now, it'll look bad for Dad. All Steele's trying to do is get back in the sheriff's race." He glared at Ty. "Some hero you are, figuring this out just now."

Ty shrugged. "I'm going to search the lockers again. I need you and Angel."

"This is so low, trying to get at my father by manipulating Laney," Thomas whispered furiously. "You ought to be ashamed of yourself."

Ty held Thomas's gaze. "This isn't an attempt to do anything but prevent a school shooting."

"If you go near the school, you're fired," Laney's father said flatly. "We both know this is nothing more than a campaign ploy."

Laney wavered. Her father was counting on her. His need projected itself clearly. The desire to please him, to gain his approval and therefore his love, filled her more forcefully than ever before. If she ran out on him now, he might never forgive her. *Please, God, help me do the right thing.*

"Come on, Laney," her dad urged. "For once in your life listen to reason."

Is my father right, Lord? She imagined the long line of her failures soaring to the sky like a kite on a windy day.

Her father seemed to sense her indecision. "You'd only be encouraging Steele to throw away what's left of his career."

Laney looked from her father to Ty. She wanted to please both of them and couldn't. Maybe her father was right. By refusing to help Ty, she'd be doing him a favor. And then she realized it didn't matter what either of them wanted for her. She needed to do what God wanted for her.

You know me, God, better than anyone. Where do You want me?

Laney opened her eyes. She threw her shoulders back and tilted her chin to meet Ty's gaze. If Rock had taught her anything, it was that if she didn't take herself seriously, no one else would either. "I'm going with you."

Her father's jaw tightened the way it always did when he attempted to control his temper. "If you walk out of here, Laney, don't plan on coming back."

"I'm going," Laney said flatly. She pulled a paper from her pants pocket and handed it to Thomas. "You'll need this."

&

"Angel's in the van," Laney said, pushing the building's glass doors open.

Ty eyed the dusty van parked with two wheels on the curb and Angel hanging out the front seat window.

Laney followed his gaze. "I parked in the shade for Angel."

"What shade?" Ty asked. "The parking meter you've nearly knocked down?"

"It's just leaning a little." Throwing open the door, she began to climb inside. "We don't have time to argue about my parking job."

Ty slipped in ahead of her. "You're right," he said, "but I'm driving. I've seen you in reverse, and it isn't pretty."

Laney climbed into the passenger seat. She kept her head held high as the minivan bounced and scraped its way off the curb. He swung the car out of the parking spot and accelerated in a burst of speed that sent Angel's ears flying. Laney braced her legs and wondered if the minivan had ever gone this fast.

Glancing at Ty's profile, Laney saw the stubborn set to his jaw and the tightness of his hands gripping the steering wheel. The reality of what they were doing slammed into her. If he was right, they were about to step into the middle of an extremely dangerous situation. Ty could be shot, possibly killed.

He wouldn't hesitate to put himself in front of a bullet if it meant saving someone. *Lord, please take care of Ty. Don't let him get hurt. If I trip or do something else clumsy, please let me trip the right person. In Your name I pray. Amen.*

"Wish I had my siren," Ty muttered as he pushed the accelerator.

"Look out!" Laney shouted.

Ty hit the brakes, and the minivan skidded sideways. "What?"

"A squirrel!" Laney shouted. "You nearly ran it down. Didn't you see it?"

"You're nuts," Ty said. He straightened the steering wheel. "Actually, I'm the one who might be nuts." Shaking his head, Ty looked directly ahead. "I'm paranoid, probably, even to think something is going to happen at the school."

You're not the only one, Laney thought, *who's suffering from paranoia.* It had to be her imagination, but she could have sworn she'd just seen a vintage red convertible following them. Why would Rock be tailing them? Had her father sent him to arrest them? No way, she decided, relaxing slightly. He would have sent his deputy in a patrol car.

"Don't worry," Laney said. She gripped Angel more tightly. "No matter what happens, we're doing the right thing."

She checked the rearview mirror once more for Rock's car and saw nothing. Of course she wouldn't see anything. Right now Rock stood in the first row listening with rapt attention as her brother introduced her father. Suddenly she had an awful thought. *I couldn't have given him the wrong paper, could I?*

What if she had? Would Thomas read the poem she'd

found in church? With a sinking feeling, she reached in her pocket and pulled out a piece of paper.

"Oh, no!" Laney blurted.

"What?" Ty scanned the road nervously and tapped the brakes. "Another rodent on the road?"

"No," Laney moaned. "I gave Thomas the wrong piece of paper. Instead of my speech, I gave him the poem." She shut her eyes.

Ty's frown increased, but he didn't have time to respond. The high school came into sight then, a sprawling red-brick building with two sides coming together in a two-story-high glass wall. He slammed the brakes as the minivan skidded to a halt in front of the school.

"Let's go," he said.

Laney gave one last look over her shoulder, scooped up Angel, and then hurried after Ty.

twenty-two

"I'm sorry," the receptionist in the front office said when Laney and Ty stopped to register in the front office, "but no dogs are allowed. It's a school policy."

Ty whipped out his badge. "That's no dog," he growled. "That's a canine officer."

The woman adjusted her glasses higher on her nose. "I've never seen a German shepherd that looked like that. In fact, I've never seen a dog with such big ears."

"It's a papillon," Laney said.

"Just give us our passes, please," Ty said. He shifted his weight. All his senses were screaming to hurry, and this woman looked as if she were prepared to spend the afternoon questioning them.

"I'll need your identification," the woman said, still starring at Angel and making no move to register them. "All of you."

Laney pulled out her driver's license. Ty handed her his badge. Wiping the sweat off his forehead, he hoped she wouldn't demand to see Angel's identification.

Finally a machine printed off two self-adhesive badges. Ty ripped them off the machine and headed for the door.

With Laney close on his heels, Ty climbed the stairs two at a time to the second floor. Bursting into the hallway, he passed students crowding the corridor. Lockers slammed, and laughter echoed through the halls. Boys in baggy jeans shoved each other playfully, and girls with hip-hugging jeans looked at Ty curiously. Ty hoped they were in time.

As they neared the locker, he stopped and signaled Laney to be quiet. The door of the locker swung wide open as a tall, skinny boy of about sixteen peered into its depths. Ty grabbed Laney's hand and pulled her into the recess of a nearby classroom door.

"What are you doing?" she whispered. Her fingers tightened around Angel.

"Just watch," Ty whispered back.

Moments later the boy finished loading his backpack. He slammed the locker door shut and turned toward the stairwell.

As the boy passed them, Ty pressed Laney behind him to hide Angel.

"Did you see what's in his hand?" Laney whispered to Ty. "It's the same lunch bag we saw last week."

"I see it," Ty said.

"Shouldn't we stop him?"

Ty shook his head. "Not yet." He silenced the next question on her lips with a glance.

They heard the noise from the cafeteria before they saw the large, rectangular room. The roar of voices talking and laughing was ordinary and reassuring. The smell of fried food that wafted through the air suggested that cheeseburgers and onion rings, not violence and shooting, were on the menu.

Laney and Ty paused at the entrance to the cafeteria

and scanned the room. Hundreds of students crowded around portable gray tables. Others passed slowly through cafeteria lines.

Floor to ceiling windows on the far side of the room opened into an outdoor courtyard area and provided a view of the surrounding pine forest.

Laney touched Ty's arm. "He's sitting down," she said, "all by himself."

Ty nodded and led Laney to the table across from the boy. Apparently oblivious to them, the boy sat at the table staring at the brown paper bag in front of him. His long, thin face held little color or expression.

"Aren't you going to do anything?" Laney looked at Ty. "Shouldn't you question him or something?"

"Just wait," Ty said.

"What if he's waiting for the cafeteria to fill up before he starts shooting?"

"What if he's just some kid who wants to eat his lunch in peace and quiet?"

"What about the corn chips? We should let Angel sniff them."

The boy had placed a large, wrapped sandwich, a can of soda, and the family-sized bag of chips on the table.

"Just wait," Ty repeated.

"Do something."

Ty frowned. "Like what? Tell him to put down the bag of chips or I'll shoot?"

"Of course not." Laney rolled her eyes. "Confiscate his lunch."

Ty frowned. "Sure. I'll tell him I'm the nutrition police."

"He isn't eating," Laney pointed out. "Surely there's something suspicious about that."

"Most teenagers don't," Ty said.

"Tell me why he's just staring blankly at the bag of chips."

Ty ran his hands through his hair. He checked his watch.

"You've got to do something," Laney insisted. "Look at his eyes. Something's wrong." She rose to her feet. "I'll just stroll over there and let him pet Angel. If Angel gets within six inches of that bag, we'll know for sure."

There was no way Ty was going to let Laney near the boy until he was certain it was safe. As she started to rise, Ty placed his hand on her arm. "Start praying for that kid if you want to help." By giving her a job, he hoped to keep her away from the boy until he understood the situation more completely.

"Okay," Laney replied.

Ty studied the boy. Sure, the kid was gawky. He'd been a bit like that himself at sixteen. He clearly remembered Mickey's razzing him for the size of his hands hanging off long, skinny arms. None of his parts had seemed to fit, and the mirror told him this most eloquently of all. Yet all kids went through this phase. And if the boy was alone, that wasn't necessarily a warning signal either.

His eyes moved over the boy and came to rest on the boy's hands. The kid's wrist bone was as awkward and protruding as his had been. The bone looked as if everything would catch on it. He wondered if anybody had ever told the boy he would grow into his bones as his brother had done for him.

As if sensing his scrutiny, the boy moved his arm. The sleeve slid back and revealed a drawing scribbled in blue ink. Ty's heart accelerated as he saw the same drawing of a bullet as the one he'd seen in the dirt. *Okay, Lord—please be with me. Here we go.*

Jumping to his feet, Ty moved in front of the boy. After a long moment of deliberate avoidance, the boy acknowledged Ty's presence. "What?"

Ty flipped his police identification onto the table. "Hand over the corn chips, kid."

The boy sneered as if Ty had insulted him. "You're joking, right?"

"It's not a joke," Ty stated.

"No way."

"I need to see your lunch." Ty kept his voice pleasant.

In response the boy pulled the corn chip bag to his chest.

"I just want to see what's in the bag," Ty said. "I want to help you."

"I don't need your help." The boy's gaze slid past Ty.

Ty's eyes narrowed. "I think you do."

The boy made a sound that could have been laughter. "You can't confiscate my chips."

"Why do you have a bullet tattooed on your wrist? Why did you leave that drawing on the ground?" Ty extended his hand slowly. "I just want to help."

The boy shrugged. "Then leave me alone."

"I will if you'll hand over the chips," Ty said, aware of how absurd it all sounded.

"What? And nobody gets hurt?"

Ty's head swung around at the voice and saw Rock Weyeth. The district attorney grinned widely at the surprise Ty worked hard to conceal. Behind Rock, Laney shook her head in obvious disbelief.

"What are you doing here?"

Rock grinned. "I followed you." He raised his eyebrows. "Really, Steele, I always knew you were a bully, but stealing a boy's lunch is a bit much. Even for you."

"Who's he?" the boy asked.

"Rock Weyeth." Rock's shoulders straightened visibly. "I'm the district attorney. Do you want to press charges for harassment?"

A bead of perspiration appeared on the end of the boy's nose and hung on, defying gravity.

Ty inched closer to the boy. "I'm on your side, kid."

"You don't have to give him your lunch." Rock circled his ear with his finger. "This guy is officially looney." He tugged Ty's arm. "Come on, Steele. You've caused enough trouble."

Ty shrugged him off. "You don't know what you're getting into here, Weyeth."

Rock gave a long-suffering sigh. "I know exactly what's going on here." His blue eyes rolled to the heavens. "You're trying to make a big deal over nothing. It's a last-ditch effort to clinch the election."

"And you're just here to make trouble for Ty." Laney stepped closer to the table.

The boy shifted in his seat with his arms around the bag of corn chips. "I'm the one leaving."

"First hand over the chips," Ty added, feeling more foolish than he could ever remember.

"Making him hand over his chips is a violation of his civil rights," Rock declared. "There's no just cause to search his lunch."

"Shut up, Weyeth," Ty said.

"Oh, dear," Laney said. She released Angel. "Fetch!" she cried.

The small dog leaped the table in a furry blur, pulled the bag of chips from the boy, and returned it to Laney.

Rock grinned. "I guess we can add assault charges to the list."

Ignoring him, Laney stuck her hand into the bag. The unmistakable sound of corn chips filled Ty's ears. He saw his entire career flash before his eyes, and for a moment, he simply stopped breathing. And then Laney said, "Oh, no."

Rock's smile widened. " 'Oh, no' as in there's a bag of chips here?"

Laney shook her head. "No. There's a gun in here."

The color faded from Rock's cheeks. "There's a gun in the bag?"

The boy said, "I wasn't going to use it. I only wanted people to take me seriously."

Rock reached for the bag. "You're joking, right?"

"I'm not joking," Laney said.

"She doesn't joke," Ty confirmed.

"Give me the bag," Rock ordered. "It's evident the two of you have lost your minds."

"Rock, stop it," Laney warned as the district attorney wrestled for the bag.

"Just give me the chips, Laney," Rock demanded.

He gave one long, hard pull. The bag ripped, sending corn chips, bullets, and a Colt .45 to the ground. The pistol clattered to the floor, and a single shot exploded through the cafeteria.

Rock fell facedown to the floor. When he turned, Laney saw a large red stain spreading across the front of his white button-down shirt. At the same time, water began to pour out of a hole in the ceiling.

Laney quickly lunged for the fallen gun as the boy struggled in Ty's grasp. Holding the gun in trembling hands, she looked down at Rock. "He's bleeding!" she cried.

"He's not hit," Ty assured her. "He landed on a bottle of ketchup."

Other students crowded around, drawn by the gunshot and the water pouring out of the ceiling. "It's okay," Ty told everyone. "There's been an accident, but please return to your seats."

Ty kept one arm on the boy, who kept his gaze trained on the ground. He had no fight in him, and Ty doubted he ever had. The boy probably had been teased beyond his endurance, and bringing the gun to school had been a way to show his manhood. In that moment, Ty resolved to find a way to help kids like him deal with the bullying and hazing that went on in every school.

For a moment, his gaze met Laney's. He saw compassion for the boy in her eyes and, as he held her gaze, something else. His heart beat faster, and he barely felt the water dripping over him as the rest of the sprinklers in the room turned on. Her eyes held all the promise of a candle burning in the window on the darkest of nights. It was a gaze welcoming home a man who had been gone for a long time. It was a look that could have lit up the emptiest, coldest house. Even his own. The look told him more eloquently than any words could express. For the first time in years, perhaps ever, he was home.

twenty-three

Laney stood holding the gun as the sprinkler system rained down on them. Across the distance between them, she anchored herself in Ty Steele's gaze. She saw a strong man who cared for others more than himself, who had been willing to risk his professional reputation, even his life, to avoid a school shooting. Her heart opened up to him.

"Please keep back," Ty ordered the crowd of students who pressed around them, more curious than afraid now that he clearly had the situation under control.

Did the students realize things might have ended a lot differently if not for Ty? Her hands shook, and she tightened her grip on the gun. Later she would let herself react to the scene; for now she would be strong for Ty.

She wasn't sure how much time had passed when she heard a familiar drawl.

"Get someone to turn off the main water switch," her father ordered. "Where's Principal Henley? And someone get the fire department out here. Step aside, kids," her father said. "Show's over."

"Dad!" Laney called.

He pushed through the row of students. "Laney, are you okay?" He looked at the pistol in her hand, and she saw the color drain from his face. "What are you doing with a gun?" He reached for the weapon. "Just give it to me slowly."

"It's okay, Dad." Laney handed the pistol to him. "Ty has it all under control."

Her father shook his head. "Then why is there a hole in the ceiling with the sprinkler system going full blast?"

"I can explain," Laney said. "You see—"

"The gun went off accidentally," Rock interrupted, "when I tried to take it away from Laney."

Water dripped down the district attorney's face. One of his contacts had fallen from his eye, giving him two different-colored irises. His normally immaculate clothing hung dripping wet, and he had a large ketchup stain on his shirt.

"What happened to you?" her dad asked.

"I hit the ground when the gun went off," Rock explained.

The older man cut him off with a slash of his hand. Turning to his daughter, he said, "You fired the gun?"

"Not exactly," Laney tried to explain.

"Laney, tell me you didn't shoot down the sprinkler system," her father said.

Laney saw the anger in her father's eyes. Under his intense scrutiny, something in her began to shrink. No matter what she said, he would see her as the source of the problem, not the solution.

She squared her shoulders and raised her chin. Her mouth formed a straight, tight line. If her father wanted to believe the worst about her, so be it.

"She didn't shoot down the sprinkler system," Ty said,

stepping forward. "Your daughter disarmed a disturbed student," he explained. "And probably prevented a shooting. You'll get a full report on your desk by tomorrow morning."

Laney's cheeks turned red. "Well, Angel should get most of the credit. We thought there were bullets in the bag. Neither of us guessed a gun was in there, too."

Her father held up his hands. "I still don't understand how the gun went off."

Rock coughed and stepped forward. "In the process of my assisting her, the gun fell from the bag of chips."

"He ripped the bag open because he didn't believe there was a gun inside," Ty explained. "It went off when it hit the ground."

Her father's gaze went from Laney to Ty. "Do you realize someone might have been killed?" He pulled at his moustache. "Laney, if something had happened to you—" He didn't finish the sentence.

"Your daughter has a lot of courage and faith," Ty added quietly.

"Laney?"

Something about the way he said her name made her turn to meet her father's gaze. For a moment, she saw something there she couldn't remember seeing in a very long time. Could it be he was actually proud of her?

"Nice job," her father said. "You, too, Steele."

"Thanks, Dad." Laney stood a little straighter.

Her father worried the end of his moustache in a gesture that Laney recognized as extreme discomfort. She almost smiled. Apparently her father was as uncomfortable at giving praise as she was unaccustomed to receiving it.

"That doesn't mean I ever"—her dad paused for emphasis—"ever want you to get involved in police business again." His hand dropped to his gun belt. "From now on, you stick to selling hamsters," he added gruffly.

"Yes, sir," Laney said and looked away from him. "One last thing—I want my poem back."

Her father shook his head. "You'll have to get it from Thomas. He started to read your speech but got all choked up." He lifted his gaze to the ceiling as the water finally stopped. "Glad somebody finally found the water valve." He didn't look at Laney. "I'd like to hear your speech sometime, though."

"Chief, what do you want me to do?" a policeman asked.

Her father frowned at the deputy. "Call in a bomb squad," he instructed. "We're going to do a locker-to-locker check. I want every backpack looked into and every student searched for weapons."

"Looks like someone heard you already," Ty said. He pointed at a small, big-eared dog splashing its way through the room toward them. "Your firearms-sniffing dog is reporting for duty." He grinned at Laney, who gave him the thumbs-up sign.

Laney watched Angel pause to scarf up a fallen hamburger floating on the water. Her father saw it, too. Although his Adam's apple bobbed furiously, he said nothing.

"Sir," another deputy said, "we're ready to take the boy into custody."

Her father cleared his throat, and the noise seemed to travel a great distance. "Okay," he said. "Get Olveriz over here. He'll go with you."

As the deputy led the boy away, her father began to fiddle with his moustache. "Would someone tell me why anyone would bring a gun to school? What did he think he was going to accomplish?"

Laney didn't like the flush that had appeared on her father's cheeks. "Dad, maybe you should take it easy—your heart—"

"It's not my heart that's the problem," he said with his usual bluntness. He turned to Ty. "You were right. I should have listened to you." He paused and extended his hand to Ty. "Congratulations. You're going to make a great sheriff, Steele."

twenty-four

Laney walked with Ty to the outdoor courtyard. Her wet hair and clothing chilled her to the bone, and for once she welcomed the heat and humidity. Plus, what could have happened if she and Ty had not gotten there in time was beginning to register.

What kind of world drove children to such despair that they would resort to such an act?

"You okay?" Ty put his arms around her shoulders and drew her onto one of the curved cement benches.

"I'm fine." Laney let Ty envelop her in an embrace. The rush of adrenaline flooding her had drained away, leaving her bone-tired. Her head rested lightly against his shoulder, the curve of his muscle forming a perfect pillow for her face.

He lifted her chin to study her face. "You're crying." He sighed, the uneasy sound of a man not comfortable with a woman's tears.

"I'm sorry."

"Don't cry," Ty said. He wiped a tear with his thumb.

"I can't help it." Laney sniffed loudly. "I'm not used to things going right. It's a new experience for me."

He laughed. "We did okay."

Through her tears she smiled. "I say we got more than a

little help from above." She saw the agreement in his eyes. "God gets the credit."

Ty nodded. "The credit is His." His eyes twinkled. "I never thought I'd be saying that again."

Laney nodded. "All because of that note I found in church." Her expression turned radiant through the tears. "It brought us together. Neither one of us could have stopped the shooting without the other."

Ty didn't disagree with her. He squeezed her more tightly against him. When she turned, she saw his head bent, as if in prayer. Her hands joined his as she added her own prayer.

Laney closed her eyes, enjoying the closeness. She was aware, as she knew he had to be, that things forever had changed between them. He had trusted her when no one else would and risked everything that mattered to him in the process.

They sat that way for a long time. When Ty gently pushed the wet hair off her face, Laney opened her eyes and met his gaze. She knew there were things unsaid between them, things that hung in the air as soft and beautiful as the scent of a rose. She did not know when the right moment would come to speak the words aloud. For now it was enough simply to sit next to each other and know she was at the beginning of something more precious and miraculous than she ever could have imagined a relationship could be.

Ty squeezed her fingers lightly. "I have something I'd like to ask you."

"A question?" Laney bit her lower lip as she took in the sudden set to his face. Her heart began to beat faster at his serious expression.

He smiled. "I want to know about the pastor's assignment."

Her brow wrinkled. "What about it? I know you weren't the writer of the letter I found."

Ty's voice was low and gentle. "I want to know about your letter. What did you write?"

Laney swallowed. The image of herself crawling around the seats trying to find her lost note because she was too ashamed for anyone else to read it flashed through her mind. "You sure you want to hear this?"

Ty nodded.

"I'm a jinx," Laney whispered. "Everything I touch turns into a disaster." She couldn't meet his eyes. "You've seen for yourself it's true."

Ty laughed.

"This isn't funny!" Laney cried out. "You're lucky to be alive. The shot that hit the sprinkler system could as easily have hit you."

Another round of laughter erupted from Ty. Laney covered her ears with her hands.

"Look at me, Laney," Ty said softly. "I'm more alive than I've been in years. Everything you said about me the first day we met was true. I knew it then, and I know it now. You haven't hurt me, Laney. You've healed me."

Laney pressed her lips together and twisted her hands in her lap. "The credit is God's. If you're talking about me, you're lucky to be alive."

"Yes, I am lucky," Ty agreed. "Although I didn't feel that way until I met you." He reached over and squeezed her hand tightly. "I have the feeling that as long as I have you next to me, that's the way I'll feel the rest of my life."

"It'll be a short life," Laney predicted gloomily, "if I'm in it."

Ty scowled. "You can go on believing that, or you can take a chance on me. On us."

Laney shook her head. "I don't want to hurt you."

Sensing her hesitation, Ty continued, "I'm strong, Laney. Strong enough for whatever happens. The only thing I can't handle is for you to walk away from me."

Laney studied the shape of their fingers intertwined. She could almost see how their hands would age, becoming more fragile, yet gaining strength from the touch of the other.

She thought about the day in church when Pastor Bruce had asked them to throw away their fears and regrets. At the time, she realized, she'd held on to her doubts about herself. Looking into Ty's eyes, she knew it was time to let go.

Laney leaned forward. "What are you asking?"

Ty swallowed. "For a chance to date you in a restaurant without your crawling away from me like GI Jane. To picnic with you at our pond. To write you poetry."

The proof of his feelings gleamed softly in his eyes. Her own eyes answered him, filled with hope and promise. As Ty leaned forward to kiss her, Laney heard the thunder roll.

Thank You, Lord. You are truly awesome.

twenty-five

Two weeks after Ty won the uncontested race for sheriff of Sutton County, an elderly woman walked into Animal Ark. The woman had pure white hair and a small pair of glasses that sat so low on her nose they seemed to be glued in place.

Removing her arm from the depths of a fish tank, Laney studied the woman. She seemed familiar. As she searched her mind for the right connection, the woman wandered over to the gerbil cages.

To Laney's amazement, the woman sighed loudly and moved so close to the glass tank her spectacles actually clinked against the tank. "Oh," the woman said, pointing. "That gerbil looks just like my Mandy."

As usual the sight of someone in distress went directly to Laney's heart. Putting her hand on the older woman's shoulder, Laney asked kindly, "You've lost a beloved pet?"

The woman nodded. Her white head bobbed, but her glasses remained in their gravity-defying position. She blew her nose into the handkerchief, folded it neatly, and repeated the action.

"I'll pour us a cup of iced tea," Laney said.

Drawing her toward the back room, Laney clasped the older woman's hand gently. The woman's bones showed clearly through her skin, so Laney took care not to squeeze too hard.

She turned to the older woman. "I'm Laney Varner."

"Diana Gibson."

Laney led Mrs. Gibson to the back of the store and cleared a bag of rabbit pellets off the desk seat. Taking a bottle of iced tea off the shelf, she poured some into a paper cup.

As they sipped their tea, Mrs. Gibson talked. She told Laney all about the various animals she'd had and loved. It was obvious the woman was lonely.

The cup of tea long finished, Mrs. Gibson continued talking. By now she'd moved into relatively recent history and begun to recount an incident ten years ago when her husband had given her a rather unusual anniversary present—a Mongolian gerbil.

"You know," Mrs. Gibson confided, "you always hear of people getting attached to their dogs and cats. Obviously they've never had a gerbil. I named her Mandy after the Barry Manilow song. When the grandchildren came, she never bit them."

Suddenly Mrs. Gibson's eyes began to swell with tears. "That's how the accident happened, you know. About a year ago, one of my grandkids was playing with her. We were letting her run laps around the inside of the washing machine. I'm afraid the wrong button was pushed."

Laney patted Mrs. Gibson's arm and muttered soft words of encouragement. "I'm so sorry," she said.

"It was all my fault," Mrs. Gibson said sadly. "I was careless with my love."

The words echoed in Laney's ears. Her mouth fell open in astonishment. "I was careless with my love," she repeated. The words matched perfectly in her brain, but she refused to believe the implications.

"It's been a nightmare living with the guilt," Mrs. Gibson added, shaking her head and blinking furiously. "Once in church, I even—"

"Wrote a poem," Laney finished.

"How did you know?"

"I found your poem," Laney said. "I picked it off the floor because I thought it was mine." Her eyebrows pushed together in sympathy. "I thought the poem was beautiful, and I tried to find who wrote it. I wanted to help."

Laney opened a drawer in her desk and pulled out the crumpled piece of yellow paper, glad her brother had returned it to her. Now she understood why the woman had seemed so familiar to her. She must have seen her in church.

"I'd like to tell you about what happened because of your note," Laney said. "God used it to work a miracle."

As Laney told her about the love she'd found with Ty, a smile lifted the corners of Mrs. Gibson's mouth. She laughed when she learned of the fruitless school search and the Eat and Go incident. When Laney finished with the troubled boy at the school, she sighed. "I can't tell you how much it means to hear of so much good that came from such an accident."

Smiling, Laney handed her the note she'd found in

church so long ago. The elderly woman folded it carefully and placed it in her purse.

Laney knew there was only one thing left to do. She led the woman back into the store and to the front of the gerbil cages. "Please," she said, "let me give you the gerbil that looks like your Mandy."

Mrs. Gibson's hand reached inside the cage, hesitant at first and then more confidently among the scurrying rodents. She gently stroked one of the gerbils' heads, and when she looked up, her smile was radiant.

Watching, Laney's heart lifted in response. If she hadn't retrieved the wrong note that day in church, none of this would have happened. She closed her eyes, filled with a profound sense of love of God and gratitude and a commitment to give back as many of the blessings she'd received as possible.

Mrs. Gibson waved gaily as she left the store with the gerbil secured in a pet box. Laney, still lost in the wonder of it all, did not notice the top of the gerbil cage was wide open.

epilogue

One year later

A soft breeze lifted Laney's veil and stirred the rose petals under her feet as she walked slowly to the man waiting for her by the edge of the church's pond. Although most of the town had gathered to witness her wedding, she had eyes only for Ty.

No music played, no bridesmaids preceded her, and no flash of any camera recorded the moment. She'd wanted it simple with none of the frills or pressures of a formal wedding, and that was just what she had.

Step by step she moved closer to Ty. As the distance between them lessened, the smile on her face widened. It wasn't that he looked so handsome in his policeman's dress uniform or with the sheriff's badge glimmering on his chest. It was the simple things—the sprig of wildflowers pinned to his lapel, the expression in his eyes, the smile that promised a life of good times and difficult ones—that melted her heart.

Oh, Gertha Williams had tried to talk her out of having the wedding here in front of the church pond. The church secretary had struggled not to appear appalled. "Wouldn't you be much more comfortable," she'd said, "in our new church?"

Laney had thanked her for her concern but held fast to her desire to marry Ty in the place where it all had begun. Gertha hadn't been the only one to question Laney's wedding plans. "What do you mean?" her father had said. "You're going to take out a full-page ad in the *Daily Destiny* instead of sending out wedding invitations?"

Even her friends had been slightly baffled.

"What are you going to do if it rains?" June had asked.

Laney had simply smiled. In the end, June had pinned her hair up in a soft bun guaranteed to survive any kind of weather.

Angel, stationed at Ty's feet, wagged his tail as Laney approached. He made a handsome ring bearer, she thought. His long hair had been brushed until it gleamed. One of her father's last acts as sheriff had been to award the papillon with a specially designed coat that identified the dog as a canine officer. On that coat her father had pinned a medal of valor for Angel's role in preventing the school shooting.

Finally Laney reached her destination. Her throat tightened as Ty lifted the veil from her face.

Someone in the audience sighed. She saw in Ty's eyes that he thought she was beautiful. And beyond that she felt the connection between them, so deep and strong it could only be a gift from God.

In the distance, sunlight broke into millions of pieces and danced atop the smooth surface of the pond. Somewhere along the banks a frog hopped into the pond and broke the silence with a loud plop.

"I guess that means we should get started," Pastor Bruce said. He smiled as several people chuckled.

As she reached for Ty's hands, Laney thought how right it all seemed. Everything was in harmony, from the frogs in the pond to the breeze on her cheeks.

Ty looked deeply into her eyes and spoke the age-old vows. As he slipped the gold band onto her finger, Laney felt a sense of wonder spreading through her.

And then it was her turn to say the words that meant so much. With calm hands, she put Ty's ring on his finger.

"I now pronounce you husband and wife," Pastor Bruce declared.

The guests began to applaud as Laney lifted her face to meet Ty's kiss. He was so tall that she had to tilt her head way back. Her veil started to slip, but Ty steadied it before it fell.

"Congratulations," Pastor Bruce said warmly.

Turning, Laney met Pastor Bruce's gaze. He grinned and seemed so pleased that she couldn't help but recall the last time he'd looked at her and Ty that way.

"Congratulations," he'd said, returning their papers to them. "You've passed the premarital exam."

And best of all, Laney recalled, smiling, they only had to take the test once.

A Letter To Our Readers

Dear Reader:

In order that we might better contribute to your reading enjoyment, we would appreciate your taking a few minutes to respond to the following questions. We welcome your comments and read each form and letter we receive. When completed, please return to the following:

Fiction Editor
Heartsong Presents
PO Box 719
Uhrichsville, Ohio 44683

1. Did you enjoy reading *The Pastor's Assignment* by Kim O'Brien?
   ☐ Very much! I would like to see more books by this author!
   ☐ Moderately. I would have enjoyed it more if

   _____

   _____

   _____

2. Are you a member of **Heartsong Presents**?   ☐ Yes   ☐ No
   If no, where did you purchase this book? _____

   _____

3. How would you rate, on a scale from 1 (poor) to 5 (superior), the cover design? _____

4. On a scale from 1 (poor) to 10 (superior), please rate the following elements.

   ____ Heroine   ____ Plot
   ____ Hero   ____ Inspirational theme
   ____ Setting   ____ Secondary characters

5. These characters were special because? _____

_____

_____

6. How has this book inspired your life? _____

_____

_____

7. What settings would you like to see covered in future
   Heartsong Presents books? _____

_____

_____

8. What are some inspirational themes you would like to see
   treated in future books? _____

_____

_____

9. Would you be interested in reading other **Heartsong
   Presents** titles? ❏ Yes ❏ No

10. Please check your age range:
     ❏ Under 18   ❏ 18-24
     ❏ 25-34   ❏ 35-45
     ❏ 46-55   ❏ Over 55

Name _____

Occupation _____

Address _____